Praise for COLD WIND BLOWING:

"The protagonist of Cold Wind Blowing, a hard-boiled detective, grapples with his own obsolescence, yet he's still determined to do his job, and perhaps find love. This cyberpunk noir novella feels like Phillip K. Dick and Raymond Chandler made a book baby and woke up in a surprisingly hopeful mood. Rollicking good fun, in a fascinating world. I'd read more any day!"

— Jennifer Pullen, PhD, author of *Fantasy Fiction: A Writer's Guide and Anthology* and *A Bead of Amber on Her Tongue*

"High-tech modifications collide with low-life society. Monsters, closed-door mysteries, and too much whiskey. This has everything you want in a 21st-century cyberpunk story. It's a great ride."

— Chris Arnone, author of the *Hermes Protocol*, *Necropolis Alpha*, and the *Things Forgotten* series

"With a hard-bitten protagonist and future-noir style, *COLD WIND BLOWING* features an exciting mystery that threatens to unravel the secrets at the heart of its snow-covered dystopian world."

— Erica L. Satifka, author of *HOW TO GET TO APOCALYPSE*

COLD WIND BLOWING

GREG LEUNIG

Denver, Colorado

Published in the United States by:

Spaceboy Books LLC
1627 Vine Street
Denver, CO 80206

www.readspaceboy.com

First printed December 2023

ISBN-13: 978-1-951393-28-1

For my wife, Bailey Ross, who encourages me when I need to get off my butt, enables me when I need a break, and feeds me tacos.

And my parents, who have devoted far too many years and far too much of their own time and money at keeping us alive no matter what the world throws at us.

CHAPTER 1

Special Agent Julius Weaver stepped slowly down the rough-hewn stone staircase from the Upper Slums into the Lower. The crisp air of Arc 1 grew a little more stale with each step down into the caverns of the Lower Slums. Upper or lower, they all used the same air recyclers, so what was it about descending that affected the air?

Detective Hallis stood at the bottom of the stairs, a gene-hound and the hound's handler beside him. For as long as Julius had known him, Detective Hallis had sported an early generation cyber-eye, chrome and red and so very *robotic* looking, in place of his left. Twenty years ago, it was cutting edge—digital display, neural recording, infrared. Now, it looked outdated—not the least because of how Hallis' aging skin sagged around and away from it. Julius could never seem to look away from that eye that always seemed to be on the verge of slipping out of the detective's face and crashing to the ground in an explosion of blood and metal.

"Special Agent Weaver, this is Officer Rodriguez," Hallis said.

She was tall and pretty, with dark hair in a high ponytail and big eyes. Very tense. He reached out to shake her hand. Her gene-hound growled at him, but she gave the leash a light tug, and it backed off. They shook hands, her grip cool and firm. "And this," she said, "is

Bear. Don't worry, he won't bite you. Unless I let him." Her face remained impassive, and Julius took a step back, unsure if it was a joke or not.

Three years it had taken Julius to come to terms with the fact that he would never make another meaningful contribution to society. He had finally found a measure of inner peace in the fact that he would live out his days being paid by the FBI to do nothing, to be a figurehead. The lead agent for the Arc 1 missing persons unit. The entire missing persons unit. A unit made obsolete by the invention of the gene-hound, a genetically engineered canine with hyper-sensitive scent glands and nodules in the nose for the direct insertion of human DNA samples. Once a sample was installed in the gene-hound's nose, a wireless device in the brain transmitted to a handheld display. The gene-hound's handler could read what the dog's nose could smell, tracking scents that were days old, or finding human subjects' miles away. The gene-hound's nose represented the pinnacle in tracking technology: In the closed confines of an Arc settlement, with everyone registered in the DNA database, gene-hound K-9 units had a 100% success rate when it came to locating missing persons and fugitives. Until, apparently, today.

"Been awhile, Hallis," Julius said.

"Just over three years," Hallis responded.

"You've put on some weight."

Hallis laughed. "Yeah, well, I'm gettin' old. And all I ever do anymore is follow these damn dogs. No need to chase a perp, we just let 'em run and follow with the hounds."

"Think we're ready for this one?" Julius asked.

"We'll find out."

Julius nodded and gestured for Hallis to lead him to the crime scene. The three stepped away from the base of the stairs, into the lower slums. The cavern roof stretched up about twenty feet into the air. Lit dimly by low watt lamps connected to the Arc's eco-engines, the lower slums existed in a permanent sort of twilight. Buildings and streets stretched away to the left and right. The pawn shop was a few blocks to the south, and they walked in that direction. People stepped indoors as the officers passed. Not necessarily bad people, but there was little love of authority down here. These people were the mud beneath corporate bootheels, who could blame them for being wary?

"Go back to the surface, cyborg," the voice of a child shouted down from the second story window of one of the hab units. When Julius looked up, the window was already shut, and the curtains drawn. He looked over at Hallis.

Stoic, Hallis walked as though he had not heard the slur. A lot of law enforcement would turn that place inside out, beat up the parents, manufacture some kind of arrest. Not Hallis, though.

"Ever think of getting that old cyber-eye upgraded?" Julius asked. "Surely the department health plan would cover it?"

"You think?" Hallis said, eyes forward, one foot in front of the other.

"No," Julius said. "I guess not unless you jumped ship and joined one of the corporate police squads."

"Not my scene," Hallis sighed through his teeth.

Julius nodded, and they walked the rest of the way in silence.

Holographic crime scene tape ringed the darkened pawn shop; the four tape projectors hummed loudly from the ground. Periodically, one of the projectors would warn pedestrians to stand clear in a loud, recorded voice.

They stepped through the holographic tape, and the voice warned them that it was illegal for citizens to enter or in any way tamper with a crime scene. Hallis led them through the front door of the pawn shop, flipping on the lights. Nobody in the lower slums could afford to buy anything, nor did they have much extra to sell. What few odds and ends the shop carried looked paltry on the great expanse of empty shelves.

"I'll drop you the case file now," Hallis said, briefly tapping a few buttons on his Personal Computer. Julius' own PCom buzzed in receipt.

"Give me an overview, I'll read it all later," Julius said, poking around the assorted odds and ends on the shelves.

"Patrick Chang, 23, works this joint," Hallis said, tapping another button on his PCom. Light flowed in a tiny cascade from the holo-display into the air, until an image of Patrick Chang, wiry and nondescript, floated in the air a few inches from Hallis' hand. "Patrick lives with his girlfriend in a small hab unit down the street. She made the missing persons report about three hours after he was supposed to be home from work last night."

Julius looked at Hallis. "You checked the cameras from inside? Nothing was stolen?"

Hallis nodded, swiping from the portrait to a holo-dimensional reconstruction of the crime scene, built from pictures taken when Arc 1 PD first arrived on scene.

"Well," Julius said, "Nothing much in here. An old LED flashlight, a couple old Holo-Station Two games, some cheap silverium jewelry. Nothing to provide a motive to a kidnapper."

"How can you tell it's not real silver?" Rodriguez asked.

"Context. I'm no jeweler, I wouldn't know silverium vs silver to look at, but I do know that nobody in the Lower Slums can afford real silver. A place like this couldn't afford to buy it, wouldn't have anyone to sell it to."

He made his way to the checkout counter. Nothing but a credit-reader and a ratty copy of the first Lunar Beach edition of the Sports Illustrated Swimsuit magazine. He grinned at memories from his adolescence and flipped through it. He found a beautiful shot of Cindy Hu, wearing a bikini that might as well have been three touches of body paint. The manmade lake stretched away from the sand, and behind that the Arcology shield of the mighty Lunar Arc rose into the air. Even beyond that floated the Earth, a shining blue-white orb. The picture was bittersweet for Julius. It was a legendary shot, a symbol for his generation. Sadly, Cindy Hu had killed herself six months ago, swallowed a bunch of sleeping pills. It was all over the HV. Julius didn't watch much holovision, so any entertainment news story that he heard about was usually a big one.

A polite cough brought Julius back to the real world. He looked up at Hallis, who continued with his overview. "Of course, we brought the gene-hounds down here once already. We gave them his DNA from the databanks, and when that didn't work, we tried some DNA from the blood at the scene, in case the databanks were wrong. The hounds never even caught a scent. As far as they were concerned, Patrick Chang disappeared into thin air right outside the pawn shop. We checked the whole Arc. Nobody has left the city either. The seals on the pedestrian level emergency hatches haven't been broken, and the only shuttle traffic has been inbound. A couple cargo deliveries. Nothing outbound except for a planned orbital launch next week.

"I assume the credit-reader wasn't hacked?" Julius said.

Hallis nodded. "Nothing stolen, no money hacked. Hell, the only person in the pawn shop the whole time Chang was on shift was Chang himself."

Julius wandered over to the back door. "So, nobody came in. Chang closed down the store and stepped outside." As he spoke Julius opened the back door and stepped out. "He locked up and started towards home." Rodriguez and Hallis followed him out of the pawn shop and into the street. He took a few steps away from the door. "And then he vanished," Julius finished, standing in the spot where Chang's scent stopped. The gene-hound began to growl the moment it left the store.

Julius looked at the blood. "Anything odd with the bloodwork?"

Hallis shrugged. "Our lab's doing a work-up, comparing his on-record sample with this one, looking for inconsistencies, or drugs, or something. I'm not holding my breath." Bear continued to growl.

"Officer Rodriguez," Julius said, "why is your gene-hound growling?"

"Sorry, sir, sometimes strange scents upset them when they don't have one specific scent programmed in." She tugged on Bear's leash, trying to silence him.

"No, it's okay. Can we learn anything else about this mystery scent?" Julius crouched near the dog.

"I'm afraid not," Rodriguez said. "I can't isolate the scent in my display without having some sort of knowledge about it that would allow me to program and install it."

As his handler spoke, Bear pulled at his leash, still growling.

"Was this mystery scent present when you initially got to the scene?" Julius asked.

Hallis nodded.

"And was it investigated at that time?"

"No," Hallis said. "You have to understand, the gene-hounds pick up extraneous scents like this from time to time. Usually, it's nothing. Occasionally it's contraband. But we had no reason to suspect any contraband in a case of this nature. You think this could have something to do with some sort of new masking drugs?"

Julius shrugged.

"Doubtful," Rodriguez said. "No technology or substance has come close to masking a person's scent to the extent that a gene-hound can't pick it up."

Julius stood up. "Well, he obviously wants to follow it. Let him."

Rodriguez looked at Hallis, who shrugged and then nodded.

Officer Rodriguez let out some more leash, and Bear pulled forward, towards the south wall of the lower slums. The three followed.

Julius caught a flash of neon blue behind Rodriguez's ear. A retro-cartoon hedgehog spun in place, stopped, gave a thumbs up and a wink, and then reset. The loop took about 5 seconds. The first LED tattoo he'd ever seen in the flesh, and this one was *good* quality. Crisp detail, multiple frames. Very expensive, and not something anyone in Arc 1 could do. The K-9 cop was not from around here and she came from money. How strange. He filed it away for later.

The holo-tape warned them again as they crossed out of the official crime scene. As they neared the wall, Bear started to bark, and it soon became clear that he was leading them to a small vent that brought fresh air into the Arc.

Julius stepped forward, pulling his folding knife out of his coat pocket and flipping it open. He squatted by the vent, taking the blade to the screws on each corner of the plate. The years had not been kind to much of Arc 1's infrastructure, and these screws had been rusted into place. After struggling vainly for a minute that felt like ten, he gave up, putting the knife away.

"Need a hand?" the gene-hound's handler asked.

Probably an innocent question. Probably didn't mean anything by it. But after three years of obsolescence, Julius Weaver was damned if he was going to ask a K-9 handler for help on his first case back. He threaded his fingers through the metal grate and pulled. A moment of resistance, and then he could feel it starting to give. With a shriek of metal on metal, the vent plate came away from the metal mount, taking ample chunks of the stone wall along with it.

"Um, never mind I guess," she said.

A year ago, he'd had Arc 1's only bio-mod surgeon replace his arm muscles with a new hyper-dense muscle weave; of course, in order to do that, they also needed to replace his arm bones with a carbon nanotube structure that could withstand the new muscle. He could crush steel; and though a knife would slash his skin, it wouldn't go deep enough to do meaningful damage. The procedure had eaten heavily into his savings. His ex-wife had called it a mid-life crisis, and his therapist had asked if it made him feel less obsolete. That was the last time he'd talked to either of them.

"That'll show her," Julius mumbled, punctuating it with a cough as the crumbling stone cast a cloud of particulate dust into his face. He turned back to the detective and the K-9 unit, expecting some form of reprimand. But out here on the edge of the world, the old order still held. He was FBI, they deferred to him. The repairs wouldn't come out of *their* paychecks anyway. He set the grate down on the ground.

"Any drugs in there, or maybe a murder weapon?" Hallis asked.

Julius started to reach into the vent, but before he could, Hallis cleared his throat loudly. Whoops. Julius had forgotten his kit in the rush to the crime scene and had forgotten protocol after 3 years of disuse. He felt the heat rising from his neck to his cheeks. Turned back to the detective and reached out his hand. Hallis grabbed an extra glove out of his own kit. Julius put it on and stuck his arm into the vent, fishing for some bit of evidence. Bear still barked and growled. Though it passed through multiple air scrubbers before reaching this point, the air inside the vent still felt 20 degrees colder than the ambient Arc 1 temperature, like sticking his hand into the freezer.

There was nothing inside. He activated the display light and recorder on his PCom, pointing them into the ducts. Empty, stretching off into the darkness. No sign of anything suspicious.

Julius sighed and rose to his feet. "Nothing there," he said. Still, Bear growled at the opening, and something at the back of Julius' mind tugged at him. He tried to zero in on it, but it escaped him.

Rodriguez crouched down to have a look herself. "Something in here's got him real upset." She looked into the darkness for a few seconds and stood back up herself. She looked at the two men and shrugged. "It's okay, Bear," she said, scratching under the hound's chin. Bear whined and looked up at her.

"Back where we started," Hallis said, returning to the pawn shop.

Julius lingered for another moment, and then followed. The three combed the shop and surrounding area for another hour, but they found not one shred of useful evidence. Only the sudden disappearance of Chang's scent and the trace amounts of blood indicated that this was the scene of a crime at all.

CHAPTER 2

Old paper advertisements plastered the walls of the long staircase from the Lower Slums back to the surface, pushing everything from the best hotdogs in Arc 1 to male enhancement pills to a woman named Luscious Lucy. Her breasts were clearly implants, except that a sex worker based in the lower slums would struggle to afford a plastic surgeon. Her lips were voluptuous and her smile sultry. It had been a long time since Julius had been with a woman. He was, he knew, widely considered to be rather ugly. His hand lingered over his personal computer while he read and re-read Luscious Lucy's PCom number. Prostitution had been legal for twenty years, but it was still frowned upon, at least in law enforcement circles. Not a smart career choice for an FBI agent that had just been assigned his first case in three years.

He turned away from the flyer just as his own personal computer began to ring. He pulled it from his pocket and answered. The PCom displayed a tiny holographic projection of the Director of FBI North America. He was an imposing man, sitting behind a massive faux-mahogany desk. Though the FBI existed as a tiny fragment of its former glory, this was still his boss's boss. Calling him directly.

"Director," Julius started. "What –"

"Special Agent Weaver," the Director said, "I just received a briefing on your case. I know you don't have a partner, and I just wanted to tell you to be careful. This case is extremely important."

"I'm thrilled you're interested in a kid from the lower slums, sir but I don't understand –"

"Frankly, Special Agent, I'm not concerned with a kid from the lower slums, and I think you know that. I am concerned that the FBI does not fail where the police department's gene-hounds have."

"Sorry sir, but you're right, I figured it was politics," Julius said, climbing slowly towards the light of the upper city. "First Arc 1 missing persons case in three years, etc. I'll do my best not to make the Bureau look bad."

The Director was silent for a moment. "Politics may well determine whether you keep your job, Weaver. And much more than that."

"Message received. I'm just headed back from the crime scene now. Is there anything else?"

"No, Special Agent. Except this. Expect that this case will lead you in unexpected directions." The Director hung up before Julius could respond. He continued to stare at the now-blank display on his PCom.

"What the hell does that mean?" Julius muttered.

The stairs disgorged Julius onto the street level of the outside, also known as the Upper Slums. Most people who lived in the sunlight beneath the dome of Arc 1 preferred the network of walkways connecting the buildings' upper stories over walking in the streets. Maybe it made them feel more important, living their whole lives as far from the slums as possible. Maybe it made them feel safe. Julius didn't have a preference either way, except that the streets tended to be faster. More direct. Today, the streets took Julius from the northwestern corner of the Arc past a number of street vendors and one gene-hound patrol. The dog smelled Julius' sidearm and started barking from down the street. The officers quickly approached him, weapons drawn. The K-9's handler squinted at a display that Julius knew was telling him the size, location, and estimated model of firearm in Julius's holster.

He waited until they asked, and then showed them his badge. They uncoiled perceptibly: tension leaving muscles; eyes, formerly narrowed, relaxing back into normal position; and gun arms dropping slowly to their sides. One of the officers read the badge more closely and laughed. "Missing persons, huh? You must be bored as hell."

Julius smiled. "Not today."

The officer shrugged.

When he got back to his office, Julius found his door open, and a man standing at the window. He coughed and the man turned around. A badge pinned to his shirt identified him as Dr. Alfred Linden, FBI consultant. Slight build, with blonde hair and shifty blue eyes, Linden had dressed in a ragged parody of business casual. He seemed too young to be a doctor of anything.

The consultant seemed to shrink back. "Special Agent Julius Weaver?" His accent placed him as being from one of the Nordic provinces.

Julius nodded. "You seem taken aback."

"Ah, I expected someone a little less... intimidating, and a little more... well, washed out. Look, if this is a bad time I can come back later."

"No," Julius said. "This is an exceedingly good time for you to explain who you are and why you are in my office."

His face glowed crimson, and he did his best to stutter out an answer. "Of course. I'm Alfred Linden –"

"I can read," Julius interrupted.

"Oh, of course," Linden said. "I'm a scientist. Or rather, I was, until the Frontier Science program decided that I was no longer an integral part of their team."

"Very interesting," Julius said. "Skip ahead to why you are here."

Linden nodded, "Right. I've been hired as a consultant to assist you with your current case."

Julius stared at him.

Linden coughed and shifted his weight from one foot to the other, looking around nervously.

"Hired by who?" Julius said.

"The, ah, the Director of FBI North America."

"Why would the Director hire a scientist to consult with me on a missing person's case?" Julius was speaking aloud; the question wasn't meant directly for Linden. He responded nonetheless.

"I wasn't informed of the nature of the case. I was hoping you could brief me on it."

"What sort of scientist are you?" Julius asked.

"I'm sort of a jack-of-all-trades, master of none," Linden said. "Emphasis on the latter," he added forlornly.

"So, the Director sent me a bad scientist to help with a missing persons case that, while mysterious, has no apparent connection to any scientific institutions. That about right?"

Linden shrugged, a pained look on his face.

Julius was weighing his options—call the director and demand that he remove the consultant or ignore the consultant and go about his business—when something in his mind clicked. Always at the strangest times. He smiled.

"What is it?" Linden asked.

Julius ignored him, and brushed past to his desk. He flipped the holo-disk on and called up Hallis' case file, skipping ahead to the holo-dimensional reconstruction of the crime scene. Linden approached the desk, craning to see the display, but otherwise silent. Continuing to ignore him, Julius found the vent that Bear had led them to, and tapped his finger on the image, zooming it in. There was a partial trail beginning at the vent and ending about ten feet in the direction of the pawn shop. It was a dark stain, like some sort of clear liquid. He stared at it. "Water?" He spoke aloud. "That would explain why it had evaporated by the time I got there."

"Why would there be a trail of water from the crime scene to the Arc ventilation system?" Linden asked.

"I don't know," Julius said. "But this case just took another step towards the bizarre. And the Director obviously knows more than he's letting on. Maybe a disgraced scientist could be of some use. Let me call up a desk for you, and we'll get you situated so I can brief you."

After calling down to the admin office, Julius decided to take a detour to the roof. He needed time to digest everything he'd seen so far.

On his way to the elevator, May Ellis, the secretary for the Discontent unit, smiled at him. "Off to the shooting range again, Julius?"

He grinned broadly at her. "Nope. Got a case. Need to go to the roof and clear my head, process everything." He strolled into the elevator, relishing the surprise on her face as the doors between them slid quietly shut. The little things in life always cheered him up.

The Law Enforcement building was average height for an older design Arc: twenty stories high. The FBI offices occupied all the space from the 7th floor to the 10th floor. Any floor above these had been bought and paid for by corporate security teams that needed to liaise with public law enforcement units. Julius was proud that Arc 1 stood among a handful of cities that had resisted completely subsuming all law enforcement functions to corporations but hated that they got the top floors. At least the roof was made available to everyone. The shrinks thought cops and agents should be able to see the sky—an important kind of therapy for law enforcement officers in any kind of Arcology.

Julius rode up to the roof now, stepping out into the roof garden. He had no idea what most of these flowers and ferns were, but they smelled nice, and soothed his troubled mind. The contrast between the summer flora and the blizzard above was stark. It must have been forty below outside the plexi-bubble of Arc 1, but the city's eco-engines kept the interior a comfortable 65 °F. Out there, on the snow-swept Alaskan tundra, nothing moved except the weather, a cold wind blowing in flurries and gusts across the barren landscape. When

Julius looked down off the roof, he saw hundreds of people walking the criss-cross of upper-level tubes from building to building. He could see bits of the streets below; plenty of people were down there too, living in the upper slums.

Arcology 1, the world's first truly self-contained, ecologically efficient city. Home to one million residents, give or take a few thousand. It was old now, thirty-one years and counting. A year older than Julius, and obsolete compared to many of the Arcs being built over the last few decades. Still, Julius loved it—clean, and relatively safe, compared to the others.

It stood as a testament to the ingenuity of the human species. When most of orbital space had become clogged with debris, the equatorial spaceports had been closed down. Couldn't launch a satellite or spacecraft through a shrapnel cloud moving at 8 km/s, after all. Arc 1 became the first city to unlock the Kessler window, a launching place for advanced craft with prototype fusion engines that could take off "north," traveling up from near the poles and circumventing the cascading cloud of orbital destruction around the planet's equatorial region. Twenty years after a cascade of destruction sparked by a terrorist attack on the major orbital construction platform known as the Forge, Arc 1 allowed humanity to once again take to the stars. Colonies on Mars and Titan had only survived because of Arc 1, to say nothing of Lunar City. Communications satellites were re-established in new orbits, and a second Dark Age had ended as quickly as it began.

Nowadays, most major corporations and national entities own a piece of the northern or southern polar regions. Couldn't be a spacefaring power without a piece of the Kessler window. Arc 1's status as a national entity made it impossible for any one corporation to totally privatize it, and so with a gold rush of privately owned polar launch facilities, the little city quickly became obsolete, a backwater spaceport for the smallest corporations or for orbital scavengers in rickety old space shuttles to take off from. The perpetual storm outside the dome certainly didn't help.

He stood watch over Arc 1, his home, and considered how the gene-hounds could have been beaten. Nothing but the most outrageous fictions came to mind. People funneled through the walkways, and more snow rolled off the bubble. Julius didn't move for a long while, transfixed as he always was by the duality of the Arc—storm raging above and ants marching below. After a time, he checked his watch. Linden would be situated in the office by now, which meant it was time to get to work.

Something icy gripped him without warning, a frozen hand tickling the hairs on the back of his neck. He shuddered. Reflexively, he checked his sidearm. He popped the magazine out: 30 tungsten-uranium flechettes. He clicked the safety off, and the magnets that would propel those flechettes at hypersonic speeds hummed comfortingly. He re-engaged the safety and popped the mag back in—all in working order. Whatever danger his gut was telling him to expect, Special Agent Julius Weaver resolved that it would not take him by surprise.

CHAPTER 3

Aside from a couple of plaques on the wall from when Julius was the over-achieving sort of agent in his early- to mid-20s, his oversized office had long stood nearly empty. Julius wasn't the nesting sort. In fact, as Julius had briefed Linden on the case so far, he had noted with surprise that with the addition of the second workspace it felt comfortable for the first time.

Behind his desk, the room's lone window looked out onto the mid-level of Alaska's only remaining city, the Arc 1 arcology. From here you could only see buildings and walkways. Julius swiveled away from it, and back to his desk.

He had managed to wrangle enough of Linden's story to learn that the scientist had been laid off by the Frontier Science program because a couple of his co-workers had stolen all of his work, and his bosses had decided that he was plagiarizing them, rather than vice versa. He'd gathered this more from subtext than from the specific context of Linden's story—the man seemed incapable of saying a positive thing about himself.

Julius looked up at him now, after countless minutes lost in contemplation. Linden sat at his new desk, PCom on and humming idly. "What about a bomb," Julius asked. "Is there some sort of device that could incinerate a human, leaving the structures around him intact?”

“Ah,” Linden started, “well, sort of. A neutron bomb would kill people and leave structures intact. However, it would undoubtedly have killed many more people in the buildings surrounding the pawn shop. And in addition, it would most certainly have left a body.”

Julius sat back in his chair and stared at the display of the crime scene. After a moment, “How about some sort of technology to shrink someone down, so they could fit into the vent?”

Linden shook his head, smiling. “No, shrink rays are not within the purview of current technology, Special Agent.” His smile became a frown. “Unless there are minds much smarter than mine learning things that I don’t know. Which I suppose is entirely possible, and indeed even probable. Still, even shrunken, poor Mr. Chang would have left a scent for the gene-hounds. So no, shrinking technology is out of the question I’m afraid.”

“Huh,” Julius said. “Maybe the vent was just a coincidence.”

“Do you believe in coincidences?” Linden asked.

“No.”

“Neither do I,” Linden said. “Well, at least not usually.”

Julius tapped a few times at the crime scene, rotating the view, looking for a new angle. “See if you can go an hour without undermining yourself, Linden.”

“Oh, sorry, I’ll try.”

“And without apologizing,” Julius added.

“Yes, nervous habit, sorry –” Linden grew silent and stared at his desk.

Julius was about to speak when his holo-disk chimed. There was the still-sweaty face of Detective Hallis. He swiped his hand through the image from left to right, connecting the call. The image now live—Hallis nodded to Julius.

“Special Agent Weaver,” Hallis started.

“Yes?” Julius said.

“I’ve got another one for you.”

"Oh?" Julius raised his eyebrows.

"I'm transmitting the case file to you now. But if you want to come down while this one's fresh, I can fill you in when you get here."

"Another missing person?"

Hallis sighed. "Sort of."

No hint of mirth on the detective's face. "What do you mean sort of?" Julius asked.

"We're at 53rd and Victory, on the far west side of the upper slums. I'll fill you in when you get here."

Julius shrugged and disconnected from the call. He looked at Linden. "Want to go for a walk, doc?"

Linden exhaled slowly. "Upper slums? The slums of Arcs are notoriously unsafe. I'm no good with conflict, Special Agent Weaver."

"Relax," Julius said. "Arc 1 is as safe as they come. Come and do… whatever sciency things you're supposed to do."

Linden nodded. He picked up his bag, a small black faux-leather thing, half briefcase and half duffle bag.

"What have you got in there, doc?"

"Sciency things," Linden replied, eyebrows arched.

Laughing, Julius pushed open the door, and the two stepped out of his office. May Ellis watched him going into the elevator. When he was in, he peeked his head out and smiled at her. "Second case of the day." She shook her head in wonderment.

The elevator spit them out on the ground floor, and they exited onto the streets. Late afternoon—the upper slums were alive with people. Julius watched as Linden tensed and paled. They took the streets south, and a little west. Julius took as many alleys as he could, relishing the stodgy young scientist's discomfort. Important to enjoy the small things in life, after all. They turned into another alley and were suddenly passing through crime scene holo-tape. The same automated voice chirped at them. A patrolman came running over, hand on his gun holster. Rookie.

Julius flashed his FBI badge, and the officer relaxed. Julius was about to demand to know where Hallis was, when he saw the chubby detective rounding the corner into the alley on the other end. Rodriguez and Bear followed, Bear barking and straining at his leash. They met halfway down the alley, which turned out to be the crime scene. There was a bit of blood spattered on the walls, an empty cardboard lean-to, and not much else.

Hallis was about to speak when Julius held his hand up. "Wait, let me guess. Homeless victim, disappeared from here not too long ago, gene-hounds can't pick up the scent, and you have a witness of some kind, who observed something creepy."

Hallis shook his head slowly. "I'd forgotten how you always used to do that."

"The homeless guy part is obvious, and so is the part about the gene-hounds not picking up the scent. But how'd you know about the witness?" Rodriguez asked.

"Nobody would report a homeless person missing. Someone must have seen him disappear, or heard something and called it in. And I can tell from the unhealthy pallor of Hallis' face that it's nothing good. The anticipation is killing me. What did our witness witness?"

Rodriguez smiled, and Hallis spoke again. "Our witness is a street vendor, sells fake watches around the corner. He knows the homeless guy, says he never talked, but that everyone around here called him Quiet Bob. He didn't see anything, but he heard..." Hallis trailed off and sighed.

"Yes?" Julius prodded.

"He claims he heard terrible screams, 'wet noises,' and the sound of bone crunching. At least a dozen bones crunching," Hallis said. "His words. 'At least a dozen bones crunching.' God knows where he got 'at least a dozen.'"

"Well, that's quite a wrinkle." Julius smiled. "A brutal murder unfolds in this alley, and we have barely got a light spritzing of blood. No body." He looked at Bear, who was still barking, and pulling at his leash. "I take it, Officer Rodriguez, that Bear is *not* hot on the scent of Bob?"

She shook her head. "By the way, the victim's name is Perry Glennwood. He's in our DNA databases, diagnosed with mild PTSD. Guess they got the mild part wrong. Had a daughter and two grandchildren in the Lower 56 that probably didn't know he'd lost his home."

The smile fell from Julius's face. Easy to get carried away with the excitement of working again, forget the human element. "Thank you, Officer," he said quietly. And then, after a moment of silence, "If Mr. Glennwood isn't programmed in, then Bear's picked up another mystery scent. What are the odds of that?"

"Not great," she said.

Julius looked at Linden. "We don't believe in coincidences, do we?"

"Indeed, we do not," Linden said.

"Oh, I didn't even see him back there," Hallis said. "New partner?"

"Consultant," Julius said. "A washed-up scientist. Dr. Alfred Linden."

Linden grew red-faced again, and Hallis wrinkled his brow. "A scientist on a missing persons case?"

"I know what you know," Julius said. "And you know what I know. The Director of FBINA apparently knows more than both of us."

Hallis shrugged, and Julius nodded at Rodriguez. She let out some leash, and with a lunge, Bear led them down the alley, around the corner, and down a second alley. Two more short turns and Julius immediately saw a fresh trail of moisture leading to a ventilation duct.

"Hang on," Julius said. Rodriguez reined the K-9 in, and they all turned to look at him. He advanced to and kneeled beside the wet spot. "I reviewed the crime scene holo you sent me, and there was a trail of what I believe to have been water leading from the first crime scene to that ventilation duct." Julius put his finger to the wet spot.

"It had evaporated by the time you called me in, but this time it's fresh."

"Another trail of water to another vent. What the hell does *that* mean?"

Julius tasted his finger. It tasted mostly like dirt. No hint of gasoline, nothing acidic. Nothing to indicate that this was anything but water. "Let's see if there's anything in the ventilation duct this time."

They followed the trail, Bear barking and straining at his leash the whole way. Cold winter air from the vent blasted Julius as he squatted before it with his pocketknife.

"You want to try to avoid ripping out the wall this time?" Rodriguez asked with a chuckle.

"A1 Engineering actually maintains things up here in the light of day," Julius said, easily removing the vent. He shined the light of his PCom in, and this time saw something. A small clump of glistening white matter.

The others craned to look over Julius's shoulder. "Is that..." Hallis started.

"Snow," Linden finished. As he spoke, he slipped past them, and collected the snow in a small glass jar.

"What are you going to do with that?" Hallis asked.

"Test it, of course," Linden replied.

"But it will melt before you ever get it to a lab," Hallis said.

Linden looked down his nose at the detective. "I am aware. And then I will see what sort of compounds or other trace evidence that I can extract from the liquid water." Linden paused, and then held the jar out to Hallis. "If you have something you'd like to do with this, by all means, be my guest."

Hallis shook his head and Linden sealed the jar before placing it gently in his bag.

Julius nudged Linden out of the way and bent down to look into the vent. Again, using his PCom as a flashlight, he peered into the darkness to see a trail of water droplets and a couple more tiny clumps of snow leading to a bend in the duct. Under the blowing onslaught of Alaskan air, Julius' face began to tingle. He rose and looked at the others.

"Crunching bones and wet noises, huh?" Julius looked at Hallis and then at Rodriguez. "Does it sound to anyone else like Bob was eaten?"

Hallis grew even more pallid. "The witness said it was all over in a few seconds. There's nothing that could eat an entire human being in a few seconds, and then crawl back into a 24 by 20 ventilation duct... And for that matter, it would have had to pass through the vent cover, or unscrew it, get out, and then screw it back in from the inside. It's just absurd." He was growing more agitated as he spoke.

Julius nodded. "It certainly is, and if you have any theory of the crime, I'm all ears."

Hallis was silent.

"Anything?" Julius asked.

"What if –" Rodriguez started, but was interrupted by the ringing of Hallis's PCom.

Hallis answered and spoke to the image of a man in a lab coat. "Yes, Dr. Sanders?"

"Nothing unique about the blood from the pawn shop. No drugs, no difference between the two samples. Mr. Chang was completely healthy when he disappeared," Dr. Sanders said.

"Thanks," Hallis said, and hung up. "You were saying, Officer Rodriguez?"

"Well," she said, "what if the snow's a red herring?"

"What do you mean?" Julius asked.

"Let's say there's someone out there who thinks they found a way to fool the gene-hounds. Maybe a sealed container that's truly airtight and would shed the scent that a person would usually leave on the outer part of the container, which would normally allow a gene-hound to track that sealed container. The person who has the blueprint for this container wants to test it, so they build a smaller, cheaper version. To test it, they pick random victims, kill them, and stuff them in. They want us to search for the person, but they don't want us to catch on about the container, *if* the container works. So, they trail snow to the vent to throw us off. A red herring," Rodriguez finished, face serious.

Julius shook his head slowly. "I suppose a secret murder box theory is no more outlandish than a tiny creature that eats people whole in 3 seconds. But still... why pick a homeless guy? If it hadn't been for that vendor, we never would have figured out that there was a missing person to search for."

"Black market organs?" Linden said, voice uncertain. "I believe that stem cell cloned organs are still quite expensive. Collecting a homeless man's kidney would be a profitable endeavor, I suppose."

"But why take the whole body?" Hallis said. "From the sound of it, our victim's organs are probably shredded by broken bones."

Hallis trailed off, and everyone stood gathered around the vent, silent.

"Well," Julius said, "Dr. Linden and I are going to head back to the office. We'll test this snow for DNA evidence. If Rodriguez is right about it being a red herring, there won't be anything unusual about it, and maybe we'll get lucky and find some trace evidence of our mysterious box builder." He looked at Hallis. "Let me know if anything unique comes up in the victim's bloodwork, or if you find anything else at the scene."

"You got it Special Agent Weaver," Hallis said.

"Good luck," Rodriguez added.

Julius beckoned Linden to follow. The two retraced their steps, heading back to the FBI offices. The possibilities churned uneasily in Julius's head. Magic box? Tiny monster? What else could it be? There had to be a logical explanation for this. But what? Nothing came to mind. Maybe Linden would find something. After all, he had to have some purpose for being here, the Director wouldn't have just assigned him to the case on a whim.

The streets seemed to stretch on and on as Julius walked. He had the sudden feeling that he was a teenager again, walking these same streets shortly after watching the Titan colony ship taking off from the Arc 1 shuttleport. The blue flame of the shuttle booster seemed to glimmer in the cold air, refracting in the plexicarbonate of the dome bubble. Carrying his parents into the upper atmosphere and beyond, the first few miles of the 746 million that they would eventually traverse in order to leave him behind. The buildings blurred and he seemed to fall into himself.

Was this the same part of the city from back then? Nothing changed in Arc 1, nothing meaningful anyway. The same gray buildings and linear thoroughfares he'd wandered through, or just the same sense of spinning, of confusion, a sense of déjà vu manufactured by his spiraling mind? The further he walked, the further he felt from his destination.

CHAPTER 4

They got into the elevator at the ground floor. Linden looked at Julius. "I *do* have a lab to work at, don't I?"

Julius pressed the button for the 7th floor. "You should have full access to the FBI forensic lab. I'll show you."

Julius led the scientist down a couple corridors, leaving him at the door to the forensic lab, before heading back up to his office. Once there, he surfed the internet idly, running web searches for research that was being done that could be applied to fooling the gene-hounds. When he found nothing, he tried running an FBI database search for other cases of the gene-hounds being defeated. Gene-hounds often failed in settings outside of Arcs. Regular cities like New York, Paris, London, Buenos Aires—these sorts of places simply had too much going on to guarantee gene-hound success. Hundreds of millions of scents, and no central DNA database.

Typically, they were used by corporate law enforcement to track down rogue employees using in-house genetic data records, but otherwise saw little use outside of Arcs. For searches of gene-hound failure within an Arc environment there was nothing. Closest he found was a case involving a construction site and a dead-end scent. Naturally the missing person was found dead in a patch of freshly hardened cement. Julius rolled his neck, the joints popping and crackling. There was just no precedent for this sort of thing at all.

After a few hours of sifting through reports, Julius looked up to see Linden, confused and huffing breathlessly, standing in the doorway.

"Well?" Julius looked expectantly at the disheveled scientist.

"Preliminary report shows a very strange combination of amino acids and synthetic compounds. I really can't make sense of it, but I can tell you that the sample points to nothing conventional. Seems too exotic to be a red herring, but at the same time I can't yet fathom what it points to. Maybe a greater mind could make sense of it...."

Julius mock-golf-clapped at Linden. "I do believe you went more than three hours without undermining yourself."

For what must have been the tenth time that day, Linden blushed in crimson.

"I suppose I did, didn't I."

Julius looked at Linden, waiting.

"Oh, oh that's it for now. I have many other tests to run, but I wanted to get you my preliminary findings right away." He paused, seemed to consider his next words carefully, and then spoke quietly. "Special Agent, amino acids would seem to point towards some kind of organism."

Julius closed his web search and leaned across his desk towards Linden. "Some kind of organism?"

Linden massaged his temples. "I'm sorry I can't give you any more than that for now. I have a lot of work to do."

Julius rose from behind his desk. "Okay, better get back to it then, doc. I have a contact from the old days I'm going to pay a visit to, see about looking into Rodriguez's 'magic box' theory."

Julius followed Linden out of the office. May Ellis smiled at him and waved. He nodded back. They were seeing a lot more of each other than usual. He'd always enjoyed walking past her desk; he enjoyed her bright red hair, puffy shirts, and pencil skirts.

The elevator doors closed on his brief reverie and the machine began to descend to ground level. Time to hit the lower slums again. Time to pay a visit to the ear in the shadows of Arc 1, the information broker Luther Fisk.

CHAPTER 5

efore paying a visit to Luther Fisk, Julius needed to prepare. Walking into a place like the Speak Easy in his usual suit with his FBI credentials hanging around his neck wasn't going to cut it. Law enforcement wasn't generally welcome in the lower slums, but certainly not in the Entertainment District. He was going to need to execute a costume change if he wanted this to be an effective trip.

The elevator in Julius' building dinged twice whenever it opened. He stepped in and pressed the button for his floor. The walls came to life, the digital display showing beautiful 20-somethings running in place, playing basketball, and screwing standing up in some Martha Stewart kitchen. They all wore the same neon green sneakers. Julius allowed his eyes to linger for a moment on the otherwise-naked blonde with her eyes clenched shut in performative ecstasy.

"WalCo Kicks! Run faster, jump higher! The only footwear you won't EVER want to take off. Oh yeah!"

The announcer's "oh yeah" had been timed with perfect synchronicity to the woman's "oh yeah," as she presumably orgasmed at the climax of the commercial. At that, the shots zoomed in on every wall to a close-up of the sneakers in question. The elevator came to a halt, but the doors would remain closed until the ad finished.

"Grab your PCom to buy now, 15% off if you order before disembarking from this elevator."

With that, the screen went white, and the door slid open. He stepped out and walked down the hallway two doors to his apartment, pressing his thumb to the keypad. The tiny little computer whirred and burred, analyzing his genetic material. Once it had confirmed that Julius was in fact Julius, the door swung open with a click.

Even though the US Federal Government had been replaced by corporations just about everywhere outside of the North American Arcs, FBI North America still found a way to pay its agents a decent salary. Julius' apartment reflected this quite nicely. In the twenty-first story of a thirty-story building, he had a great view of the city to the west, and the dome bubble above.

The space was definitely snug, even for a studio, but space came at a premium in any Arc. Especially in the Upper City of Arc 1. As the door closed behind Julius, the lights came on and the room computer welcomed him home in her silky voice. His usual feed sprouted from the holo-projector on the far wall. News feeds, ads for the latest firearm tech, law enforcement memes, and the latest from his favorite porn streams all danced in the air in front of his couch.

"Feed pause," he said. No time for perusing today; today he had a case. A mission. Gear up, dress down, and get to the Speak Easy.

CHAPTER 6

Black jacket, black synth-denim pants. A ballistic fiber black T-Shirt, the only nod Julius could make to protection without giving himself up as a cop. This time when Julius stepped down into the Lower Slums the flow of people did not part around him. Teens vaping on doorstops did not step quietly inside and close the door to him. He was blending.

He waded through a river of people, invisible in his anonymity. Arc 1 automatically dimmed the lights at 1930 hours to simulate night, but in this, the Lower Slums Entertainment District, the night was bright. Holo-ads and street signs showered the rough-cut low stone ceilings of the Lower Slums with neon light. Mild corp-legal drugs, adult dancers, sex shows, Real-D Parlours with neural feeds ranging from snuff (all corp-legal executions of course) to orgies. Normally, his badge would mute ads within 20 feet, but Julius had of course left the badge at home for this excursion. He wasn't here to arrest anyone; he was here for information.

Outside the Speak Easy, an Upper City suit leaned in close to a street walker. His grey jacket and loosened tie clashed with the bright pinks and purples of her one-piece faux-leather leotard. She undid the zipper halfway, revealing a bounty of cleavage. For a moment, Julius thought the man was going to shove his whole face in there.

She leaned in to whisper something to him, he nodded, and she grabbed him by the tie, leading him down the street—presumably towards the row of by-the-minute hotels half a block down.

For a moment, Julius envied the corporate drone. Never mind the very real odds that he would be one of half a dozen or so men and women to wake up missing non-essential organs in an ice bath this month; if he hadn't rolled proverbial snake eyes with his choice of companion, he was going to have one hell of a night. Girl like that probably had some fun toys installed beneath the skin. Julius had not allowed himself to have a night like that for a long time.

He signed, returning his focus to the task at hand. Tonight wouldn't be the night to start. Shit to do, missing persons to find. He opened the exterior door to the Speak Easy and stepped in.

The scream of a thousand holo-ads gave way to the murmur of muted conversation, the gentle clink of ice on glass and glass on wood: Inside, the Speak Easy purred. What always struck Julius about this place was the understated wealth of it. You didn't expect an establishment like this in the Lower Slums. Faux wood paneling on the walls lined the room, all deep mahogany; set off with burgundy carpeting.

On the left side of the room, a long bar boasted a classic setup. Tall stools and glass shelves displaying rows of liquor bottles behind a buxom bartender. On the right side of the room, an equally long bar featured a series of bins filled with assortments of leaves, pills, and powders. In either corner stood a number of teuthologic contraptions: bulbous glass bases protruding with long canvas hoses like tentacles, metal tubes and ash trays rising in some cases a foot from the bulbs. A retro way of smoking known as Hookah. The menu above the equally buxom bartender seemed a labyrinth of options. Patrons could smoke any variety of retro (and often still illegal) drugs. Straight ganja, coca-laced marijuana called bazooka, black tar heroin. Flavored tobacco if that was more your speed. The bartender would stoke a Hookah for you, or hand-roll you a cigarette, joint, or blunt. If smoke wasn't your flavor, she would serve you tabs or pills of various retro psychedelics, inject you with the vial of your choice, or serve you up with any of a half dozen other mind-altering substances.

The Vice branch of FBINA could have a field day here, though they never would—too many tax dollars flowing through; the city government needed the money. Too much muscle, too: The place boasted not one, not two, but three bouncers, each heavily augmented. Word on the street had it that there was also at least one gun-turret installed in the wall near the entrance, and Fisk certainly had goons galore in the back rooms.

It would take a rapid response team of a dozen people to take down this place, and there would be casualties. Best to let the people of the Lower Slums have their distractions.

Julius edged further into the Speak Easy, past the bouncer closest to the door. The man towered over Julius at close to seven feet, flexing chrome cyber-arms with coiled carbon/titanium alloyed muscles that could block bullets or pile-drive some poor slag deep into the pavement outside, vaporizing his skull in the process. Quite the opposite of Julius' discreet bio-augs, this bouncer's arms were no less lethal.

A hint of yellow flashed in the bouncer's eyes as he stared at Julius. Some sort of scan. The bouncer seemed to look directly at Julius' concealed firearms—first at the one in the shoulder holster beneath his jacket, and then at the smaller sidearm in his ankle holster. The giant didn't say anything, just patted his own lethal-looking weapon—a gauss submachine gun that could spit out a dozen magnetically-propelled flechettes in a microsecond, making a red mist of Julius or anyone else in the club. The message was clear. *I know you're armed: it's okay, but don't make any trouble because mine is bigger.*

Julius scanned the place, formulating a plan. Luther Fisk would probably not be glad to see him, but the man wouldn't want to risk violence against an FBI agent—he lived in a place of precarious power and wealth, a sort of symbiotic state with the authorities in the city where everyone left everyone else alone and everyone profited for it.

Some of his patrons might not exercise such discretion, however. It wouldn't do to get made as a cop by the wrong party.

Mostly, people kept to themselves. The place was all corners—long booths along the wall, some VIP capsules with privacy curtains augmented by noise cancellation weaves. Small clusters of shadowy forms huddled together, wisps of smoke circling their heads in the Speak Easy's dim light. Nobody sat on the upraised tables in the middle of the room. Every last skeever in the joint had to sit with his back to the wall, in case the wrong person came looking.

At the far end of the club, sitting by himself at a booth in the VIP section, a man watched Julius with glowing white cyber-eyes. Most modern cyber-eyes were designed with artificial pupils to soften the unnatural look, but not these; these were not designed for diplomats or factory workers who lost their vision in accidents. This particular model was famously used mostly by corporate fixers and black ops teams. Pure form over function, maybe with an element of disarming intimidation. By now, this person had no doubt identified both of Julius' weapons, scanned his face and IDed him in the Arc 1 law enforcement database, logged his body temp and heart rate, and identified his ancestry based on bone structure and skin tone.

Julius could feel his hand fluttering, torn by the urge to flee or draw his pistol and start shooting. Nothing good would ever come from this kind of attention, especially not in the Speak Easy with no badge and no backup. A split second and he decided on fight over flight—Julius Weaver was never one to back down from a challenge. He took a step towards the white-eyed man in the corner, but before his fingers could close on the grip of the gauss pistol in his shoulder harness, one of the bouncer's colossal metal hands came to rest roughly on his shoulder. "Mr. Fisk will see you now," the bouncer said.

That hadn't taken long at all. Julius let out a breath he didn't know he'd been holding, forced his hand out of the folds of his jacket, and turned to follow the bouncer into the back room of the Speak Easy.

CHAPTER 7

"You spotted me pretty fast," Julius said. "I thought I might have to have a drink and ask the bartender to get word back to you."

When Luther Fisk grinned at you, it was all platinum in there. He steepled his fingers together and leaned back behind his giant mahogany desk (this one was real mahogany, too, a priceless artifact more at home in a museum than a gangster's office).

The man exuded a kind of style from another era. From diamond earrings glimmering on both ears, to a maroon suit that looked to be silk, to gold or platinum rings on each finger; 20th and early 21st century collectibles covered every available piece of personal real estate on Luther Fisk. Most people with Luther's kind of money flashed it with cutting-edge augs and body-mods. Classically tailored suits from modern fashion brands like LuxoCorp or AZPlatinum. Not Luther, though.

When Luther spoke, his voice boomed in a deep baritone. Julius had always wondered whether that was his real voice or an affectation. "Doesn't take much to spot a fed playing dress-up in my club. Where he doesn't belong."

Julius had expected this sort of thing. He'd had cause to question Luther Fisk a few times back in the old days before the gene-hounds, and Luther ruled from a place of power. Soft words and sweet-talking were not his deal.

"Okay, Luther, enough flexing, don't you think?" Julius finally got around to sitting down in one of the chairs across from Luther. "It's me."

Unlike the leather-cushioned, tall-backed chair Luther sat in, the "guest" chairs were small and rickety. Intentionally uncomfortable. Loudly advertising the power dynamic at play.

"You know I can't touch you and I know you won't touch me. Can we move ahead to the next phase of the game?"

Luther meticulously withdrew a cigar from a carton in one of his desk drawers; cut the tip using a very old, very gold cigar-cutter; and slowly lit it using an actual wooden match from a great big carton on the edge of his desk. He puffed theatrically a few times, and then blew the smoke up into the air, watching it curl towards the low-cut stone ceiling. "Fine," he said at last. "What is the next phase of the game? Why are you here?"

"I got a case." Julius let the words twist in the air, tangling with the smoke from Luther's cigar. He studied Luther's face for any twitch or turn, but it remained frozen in that half grin. The perfect poker face.

"Isn't that what Feds do?"

"Well, I flatter myself, Luther, that you remember me from the old days before the gene-hounds. That you might remember me as a being in Missing Persons. Looking for a country girl out of place in the city, missing from your club one night and never found. But I know that even if you forgot all about little ol' Special Agent Weaver, your boys out there scanned me. And I'm sure you've got access to the public database of law enforcement personnel in Arc 1. So, you know what kind of cases I get, and because you are a savvy criminal mastermind, you know that nobody has ever fooled a gene-hound in Arc 1. Period. Meaning I haven't had a case for a really long time."

"So, what, you think I had this missing person kidnapped?" Luther leaned forward—bulging biceps flexing against his silk suit jacket, brow furrowed slightly despite the grin that now seemed to be plastered onto the crime boss's face.

"No, not anymore." Julius stood, adjusting his jacket. "Thanks for your help, Luther."

He slid past Luther's personal bodyguard and out the door, back into the Speak Easy. It had been all too clear that Luther was clueless. Julius remembered his last case too well, had relived his interactions with Luther a thousand times. If Luther Fisk had that kind of technology, he would have taunted Julius. Mocked him, relished the advantage. Like before.

Instead, he'd tried to play it cool—too cool. The stark contrast between his half-grin, his cigar, and the tensed muscles and furrowed brow proved it. Luther Fisk was flustered. That meant not only that he didn't have the tech himself, but that he didn't know it existed until Julius brought it up.

It was time to make a quick exit now, while Luther was reeling. Before the big man began to question Julius instead of vice versa. That would be a highly unpleasant conversation. If a rival outfit had found a way to fool gene-hounds, Luther would have to find out who and then find a way to steal that tech, or risk becoming totally obsolete.

Fortunately, the corp-creep with the white eyes had departed while Julius was in Luther's office. Julius did not stop to scan the other tables for him. He did not linger at the bar. He walked directly for the exit. The giant bouncer with the chromed arms stood between him and the door. This time the man did not move aside for Julius.

"You planning on abducting a Fed in front of all these patrons?" Julius asked, his voice a whisper.

The burly bouncer gave it a moment's thought. But whether it was a subvocal command from Luther or just uncertainty, the man eventually stood aside to allow Julius to exit the Speak Easy.

When Julius stepped out onto the street, he made directly for the nearest stairs to the Upper City. That little sojourn had been fraught, but fruitful. Luther knew all the major players in the Arc. Knowing that none of them had some kind of magic box meant that there was

someone new on the scene—or something unexpected at work. It
narrowed down the search, and that was something.

CHAPTER 8

When Julius returned to the Law Enforcement Building, he found it mostly empty. The street cops, of course, had a significant night rotation. But above that, FBINA offices tended to sit empty most nights. Still, a few agents burned the midnight oil, pouring over files at their desks. Julius was more interested in the lab. And whether Dr. Linden had found anything else. He didn't seem like the sort to go home when he had a puzzle.

Sure enough, Julius found the scientist hunched over a microscope, making notes with his free hand while he adjusted the focus.

"What do you have for me?" Julius asked, letting the door to the lab shut behind him.

Linden almost knocked the microscope off the table, falling back in surprise at being spoken to. Julius laughed, long and hard. Eventually the doctor joined with a few chuckles.

After the laughs died away, Linden shook his head. "I triple checked my results, because the most obvious explanation is that I screwed up."

"Seriously," Julius continued. "What'd you find?"

"Okay." The scientist took a deep breath before gesturing at the microscope. "I found a compound unlike anything I've ever seen before. It's got elements of things that are common to Earth. It's got graphite, it's got a chemical compound used in variable shock absorbers for automobiles, and some sort of carbon-based polymer. As I mentioned before, I detected trace amounts of amino acids. Strangest of all, I managed to find a faint trace of fluoroantimonic acid."

Julius looked blankly at him.

"Okay," Linden said, shaking his head. "Here goes, I guess. If I were to design an organism that could go pretty much anywhere, I would make it out of this stuff. It's a liquid, viscous, but thin enough to flow through the cracks in a doorway... or the slits in a ventilation duct covering. But if you run an electrical current through it, it temporarily hardens. So, an organism composed entirely of this liquid could theoretically travel up a wall by pushing itself up slowly, hardening as it went, and then from the top of the wall pulling itself over by becoming liquid once more."

Julius nodded slowly, still staring at Linden. "What are you talking about?"

"I'm talking about a highly advanced composite manufactured by humans in a lab somewhere that seems to speak to an artificially constructed organism."

About three months in as a ward of the state, young Julius Weaver had received a small data packet transmitted on a tight-beam laser from Titan. His parents had landed at the colony site and were preparing to disembark to begin their new lives. They wished him well, and hoped he would follow when he came of age.

That wasn't right. They had left him on the streets of Arc 1. They hadn't even had the decency to leave him at home in Houston. They had dragged him to the spaceport first, abandoning him as casually as they might toss aside a half-lit cigarette when the hostess at the Outback called their table. No minors allowed on the Titan colony.

They hadn't even done the research before packing their bags and selling their home to leave the planet.

He remembered his mother's tears, a brave smile, and a kiss goodbye. This wasn't right. The shuttle was supposed to crash on the surface of Titan, everyone dying in the wreckage. Now he had to live knowing his family was having some grand adventure at the edge of the Solar System, him a poor foster kid with one bag of clothes to his name. How could he be an orphan if his parents weren't dead?

Julius would never forget that "off" feeling, like the world was out of alignment. And now here came Linden talking about liquid organisms, and the feeling came bubbling up from 25 years in the past.

"You realize this is insane, right?"

Linden nodded. "That's why I tripled checked my results. This compound is either alien or engineered, and beautifully. I wouldn't normally hypothesize that it comes from an organism, except that the presence of amino acids would be totally extraneous to a non-organism. And further, it would support what you said earlier. About that homeless man being eaten."

Julius shook his head, bewildered. "So now you're saying that we have an ooze monster that could be eating people? Why?"

"Well, ooze monster? I don't know about your phraseology."

"Stick to questions then, why would an ooze monster eat people?"

"The same reason any other organism eats. Hunger," Linden said.

"But an ooze monster wouldn't have a stomach, would it? How could it be hungry?"

Linden shook his head. "No, look. Hunger is a biological response to the need for energy. When we're hungry, it's because our body needs more sugars to break down into fuel. Hunger is simply our word for a need to consume organic matter and convert it to energy."

"Okay," Julius said slowly. "So, your hypothesis is that an ooze monster is eating people, and converting them to amino acids? And breaking them down to generate electricity to move itself by running a current over various parts of its ooze body in order to temporarily harden them and pull itself along?"

Linden was silent for a moment, and then, "Yes, I suppose that is my hypothesis. This compound is too advanced to be used for something as inelegant as a red herring. And I can't fathom another purpose for it."

Julius nodded. "Okay. So, assuming I accept this hypothesis instead of the organ harvesting 'magic box' theory, how does this ooze feed? It sounds as though it would have none of the features of any sort of animal I'm familiar with. Like teeth."

"That's where the fluoroantimonic acid comes in," Linden said.

Julius shook his head, putting both hands to his temples. "The what?"

"It's a super acid. Far more caustic than sulfuric acid. Could dissolve a person very rapidly if applied properly."

"Applied *properly*?"

"I would guess that something of this nature would feed in the same manner as an amoeba. First it surrounds the food source; then it would secrete the acid, applying it uniformly to the food source, thereby breaking it down into a liquid; and finally, it would absorb that liquid."

"Fine," Julius said. "But why would there be crunching noises, and bits of blood at the scene? There were no hints of acid in the blood spatters, or anything else that would support the idea that the missing persons were... liquefied."

Linden shrugged. "I suppose if the organism could constrict powerfully enough, it could crush the food source as it dissolved it, which would increase the surface area exposed to the acid, thereby increasing the rapidity of the 'eating' process." He looked around the room, as if looking for some other explanation on the walls of the lab.

"The whole idea is ludicrous anyway," he continued. "And I have no idea what sort of mechanism could serve as a brain. I just can't seem to come up with any other explanation for this particular compound."

Julius nodded slowly. "Ludicrous indeed." He paused. "This explains the vents: your ooze monster is traveling through them. Between them and the outside. But why would it choose to go outside? It's over 40 below out there. And why is it tracking snow in?"

"Ah, yes," Linden said. "I almost forgot. That's the other reason I latched onto the idea of the creature moving by passing a current over itself. The colder the environment, the better the conductivity. The cold wouldn't have any adverse effects on an organism of this composition at all and would allow it to conserve a great deal of energy. The hotter its environment, the more energy it would lose every time it moved. And the organism itself wouldn't generate a meaningful amount of body-heat, so snow would cling to it, only being shed from its back when the relative heat of the vents started to thaw it."

Julius was silent for a time. He didn't believe in monsters, but no other theory explained even half of the evidence. Plus, the Director had told him to expect the case to take him somewhere that he did not know existed. "Ooze monster" fits that description pretty effectively. "The Director," Julius said suddenly, and Linden started.

"Excuse me?" Linden asked.

"The Director knows something. Can you go over the compound one more time, see if you missed anything?"

Linden nodded. "I very probably did miss something."

Julius pulled out his PCom. "I'm going back to my office to see what sort of information I can extract out of the Director."

CHAPTER 9

The Director had been a dead end. Or rather, the Director's assistant had been a dead end. The man proved to be an insufferable jackass. The Director was unavailable, but the worm of a man had refused to say why. Had refused to take a message from "a useless department staffed by a country bumpkin in a land of country bumpkins." Julius had some choice words to say about the worm-man's parentage if he thought that living in the world's first Arc made anybody a country bumpkin, at which point the assistant hung up.

So, Julius went over the FBI's head, to a higher authority. Specifically, the corporations. More specifically, BioMart. He had a buddy pretty high up in their private security division over there, figured he might know what was up. The holo-disk rang twice, and the well-scarred face of former FBI agent Marcus Spencer blinked into reality above Julius' desk.

"Julius, how are you, man," he said.

Marc was just sitting down at a desk, pouring a disturbing amount of sugar and cream into a steaming coffee mug.

"Glad to see that some things never change. Like how you prefer having dessert to having real coffee," Julius said.

"With *my* healthcare plan this doesn't even phase me anymore. When are you going to come out here and get a real job with me?"

"I have a real job. I even have a real case," Julius said.

Marcus raised his eyes and cocked his head. "Oh yeah?"

Julius just laughed, and stood up to stretch.

"A real case, huh?" Marcus said. "Is that why you're calling me? It makes you nostalgic for your old partner?"

"Remember back when New Frontiers was press-ganging Arc 1 citizens onto colony ships back in the old days?" Julius said.

Marc sipped his coffee, cradling it in his weathered hands. "How could I forget charging across the tarmac as the countdown boomed out of the loudspeakers? We pulled a dozen drugged out people from the hold of that colony ship."

Julius sat back down cracking his neck and looking pointedly at his old partner. "Yeah, I am nostalgic for that. For protecting people from corporate goons that do whatever they want."

Marc sighed. "So, are you calling me to accuse me of selling out or calling me to ask me to use my power as a Biomart security chief to help you?"

Sometimes on calls like this, Julius found his attention wandering down to the bottom corner of the holo-projection, the picture that showed you what you looked like on the call. This was one of those times. He stared at his own face, not exactly misshapen, but crooked. Eyes slightly different sizes, teeth skewed just a bit when he smiled. He'd mostly come to terms with his appearance, but every now and then he felt a bit like a monster.

"Yeah, okay. Not much I can say to that, except I *do* need your help."

Marc set his coffee down and leaned in. "I know why you stayed when I left, no hard feelings, Julius. I'm happy to help you if I can. What's up?"

"It's a weird one, Marc. Without going too much into detail, we have an unknown material that looks like a piece of some kind of ooze monster. Something partially organic that would 'eat' by dissolving and absorbing people. Do you know any corporations that are doing that kind of research? If someone has a rogue experiment, it sure would be nice having their support while we reel it in."

"Did you say *ooze* monster? Is this call a prank, Julius? That's not really your style."

"I'm dead serious," Julius said. "You know this wouldn't be the weirdest corp research happening in our world today, if true."

Marcus shook his head. "I'll ask around, see what I can find out, but it doesn't sound like anything my people do. It doesn't sound like anything that could be remotely construed as legal under the Global Charter. You know our people get just about free reign to do whatever they want, but something that eats humans for food... well, I'll see who has bio-weapons contracts out right now, but otherwise it's nothing anyone will admit to."

Julius nodded. "I don't have high hopes, but I'm desperate. If you find anything, I'll owe you one."

Marcus grinned. "You already owe me two, so if I find something you'll owe me three."

Julius laughed. "Thanks, Marc."

"You got it buddy."

Marcus' face blinked off and then the office was quiet again. Julius didn't have a lot of hope that his ex-partner would be able to find anything. Corporations weren't usually keen to work with Federal authorities, even indirectly. He was pretty much on his own. Well, except for the Nordic scientist, who was quickly proving to be a brilliant asset.

There wasn't much else to go on except for the lab work, so Julius stood up. Might as well see what Linden had come up with down there on the seventh floor. Two hours was enough for groundbreaking research, right? He was halfway out the door when the holo-disk rang again.

Hallis' perennially sweaty face grimaced at Julius from above his desk.

"You need to shower more," Julius said.

"There's been another one," Hallis said. "You're not going to like it."

From Hallis' face, from his failure to rise at the little jab, Julius knew it would be bad news, so he kept his mouth shut and waited for it.

A face replaced Hallis on the HV. "This is our latest vic, Petyr Franklin," Hallis said. "He was on a date in one of the Alaskan viewing bays on the fifteenth level, Northeast side of the Arc, when about a dozen witnesses saw a small-sized piece of black..." he heaved a deep sigh before continuing, "*goo* drops on him from the ceiling of the viewing bay. Apparently, according to all of the witnesses, the goo sort of parachuted out as it fell, and completely enveloped the vic. It constricted rapidly to the tune of crunching bones, and then seemed to dissolve Petyr and slither away in a flash. The whole thing apparently took less than ten seconds."

Hallis' face returned, and Julius thought the man looked paler than usual, though it was hard to tell through the shaded green of the holo image.

"Well," Julius said, "that's gruesome and I'm sorry to hear about Petyr, but in some ways it's good news. That actually confirms a very bizarre theory that Dr. Linden had, that I didn't think could possibly be true despite being the *only* theory. It's frightening, but now we can get down to figuring out how to capture or destroy this thing and trace it back to someone human that we can arrest."

Hallis shook his head. "I haven't gotten to the bad part yet."

"Well get to it then." Julius's heart sank.

"The vic' was a low-level accountant at the WalCo offices here in Arc 1."

Julius said nothing.

"Agent Weaver, they're going to take over this case now that a corporate employee's been killed," Hallis said.

"I know, damn it," Julius said. "Have you informed them yet?"

Hallis shook his head. "Fuck 'em, I say. They always find out without my help, so why waste my breath?"

Julius nodded. "Good, so we might have a little bit of time left. Meet me at the crime scene and let's see what we can find. I'm not giving up my first case in three years without a fight."

47

Chapter 10

Julius and Linden met Hallis and Rodriguez at the base of the elevator to the viewing bay. Hallis' demeanor told a very clear story.

Damn. The WalCo people were fast.

"I'm sorry, Agent Weaver," Hallis said. "They already took over the crime scene, nothing I could do."

Julius shook his head. Between him and the elevator to the viewing bay stood two men wearing black suits and black-lensed digi-glasses. If you looked real close, you could see data scrolling across them. Considering that LCD contact lenses could do the same job, Julius had always found the big sunglasses to be superfluous. Intimidation tactics. He stepped up to the larger of the two and looked him directly in the eyes. What he saw was himself, reflected back in the mirrored coating of the lenses. Julius Weaver. He was a big man too, and strong. He flashed his credentials.

"Special Agent Julius Weaver. This is my case, let me up."

The men looked at each other, and the larger one spoke up. "Sir, perhaps you're unaware, but the victim was an employee of WalCo. Making this WalCo's jurisdiction. You know how it works, Special Agent."

The way he said "Special Agent," emphasis on the word "special," made it sound like an insult. He resisted the impulse to strike the man in the face, and forced a smile instead.

"This is my first case in three years, and the Director of FBINA has taken a special interest in it. I'm not trying to take over, but I want in. You and I both know that there's no formal law allowing your people to take over. If I make a stink, it'll generate weeks of paperwork for your boss. Might still be his case when that's all over, but don't you think he'd rather just let me up than wade through all that bureaucracy?"

The man stared for a moment, face blank, and then his lips moved. Subvocalized communication, implants in his face picked up the words he mouthed and transmitted them to his superior. Very expensive tech. Julius swallowed and hoped he hadn't overreached. He didn't dare look back at Hallis, Linden, and Rodriguez, for fear of the looks on their faces.

After a moment, the man stepped aside and gestured at the elevator entrance. Julius stepped into the car and turned to look at the rest of his people. Linden was pale as a ghost, but he followed. Ever the scientist, his curiosity trampled his fear. Hallis stood, indecision plain on his face. Rodriguez waited on her boss, face impassive. And of course, Bear, oblivious to the interplay of politics but keenly attuned to the emotions of his master and friends, growled at nothing in particular, hackles raised.

Best not to put Detective Hallis or Officer Rodriguez in career jeopardy on his account, Julius decided. They were good cops, and if this all went to shit, he didn't want to drag them down with him. He hit the UP button, but before the door could close, Rodriguez handed Bear's leash to Hallis and wedged her hand in. She pried the doors partway open, and slid into the elevator car, standing beside Julius as they shut. He looked at her and she looked at him. "I want to see this through, Special Agent. Three people are dead."

"Glad for the backup, Officer," he said, resting his hand on the plexi-window of the elevator. As the car slid its way up the interior face of the northeastern side of Arc 1, Julius watched the snow outside. It swirled and whipped around in the wind. It howled, or so he imagined. There were no cracks in the plexi-bubble, no holes through which to hear it howling, but you could *see* it.

This particular storm, dubbed the Great White Spot by residents of Arc 1, had been raging for nine months and showed no signs of abating. There were various theories about rising global temperatures, changes to the Polar cell, and human experimentation, but no decisive answers. It seemed a constant blizzard, when in fact it was mostly just a windstorm. The annual snowfall had not differed too terribly from previous years, but the winds gusted so powerfully that the snow was constantly being churned loose from the ground, only to plummet again as though fresh snowfall. To the residents of Arc 1, their home had become a great inverted snow globe, perpetually shaken by an invisible giant.

The storm's stark beauty appealed to Julius, and he wasn't the only one. Visits to the viewing bays were up by almost 50% since the storm started. Until now, at least.

The elevator doors opened onto a full viewing bay, populated mostly by WalCo technicians and agents. A dozen CSIs swabbed the room for samples. A cluster of three gathered around the small blood-spatter in the center of the room, where the victim had been consumed by the ooze monster. Investigators in black suits interviewed about a dozen witnesses in different corners of the room. The operation was huge, compared to the four-person team that had formed between Hallis and Julius' respective departments.

When Julius, Rodriguez, and Linden stepped out, they were greeted by a very tall man in a black suit. This one didn't have the digi-glasses. Instead, he had his eyes. All-white eyes that looked through you. Eyes that saw not just your outer flesh and inner heart, but your whole presence in the world—social media data, feed data, yes, but hidden data too. Browsing data, sealed criminal records, psychiatrist's notes. Eyes that looked past you and deep into your digital soul. Everything that you were in the world stripped bare on a sub-retinal display. These were the eyes from the Speak Easy last night, there could be no doubt. This Walco agent had been in Arc 1 *before* the death of Petyr Franklin.

His demeanor said "boss," and he was vocalizing commands into a PCom rather than the newly implanted sub-vocal tech that his lackeys below were outfitted with. Strange. His graying hair would have put him in his fifties at least, but his face was smooth, sculpted; his was the objectively handsome face of a thirty-something actor or model. Most people would have dyed their hair, but then most people would have gone for cybernetic eyes that looked human.

This guy wanted you to know what he was. This guy was an Immortal. Age-stasis. Julius measured his breathing with internal beats, a meditative technique to keep himself calm, to keep the pitter-patter of his heart steady. This man could gun the three of them down right here in front of 40 witnesses, and through the sheer power of his massive wealth, walk away unscathed.

He looked angry.

"Well get me in touch with someone in the Ops department who *can* close the vents down. You have five minutes to make it happen, or you're out of a job." He waved his hand over the PCom, and then spoke again when the little holo-projector flicked on. Julius recognized the face of Kal Lamden, CEO of WalCo. From here, Julius couldn't hear the audio on the other end.

"Yes, Mister Lamden, I'm here now, and I'll take care of everything." There was a pause. "Yes, sir." Another pause. "Yes, sir." The call ended and the Immortal looked up, those eyes turning once again on Julius.

"I get it, Special Agent Weaver. You get your first case in years. It's strange and mysterious. Three people are dead. You want to prove to your superiors that you still 'have it.' You think you have something to offer me. One or all of these things are true, or you would not have risked your career so brazenly. But let's get one thing straight. This is no longer your case, and you have nothing to offer me. Because I like your hutzpah, I will allow you and your people to observe these proceedings in the corner over there, which as it is, stands against my better judgment. When you leave, you will at least have the satisfaction of knowing your city is safe once more."

Before Julius could respond, the man turned away and flicked his PCom on again. Julius was stunned into silence. Part of him roared angrily to attack this audacious man, take him down a peg or two; instead, he stood meekly in the corner. He didn't want to lose his job, and he *did* want to see the resolution, even if he wasn't the one doing the resolving. The angry part of him cried "cowardice!" but he ignored it. He had Rodriguez and Linden to watch out for, too, didn't he?

The Immortal spoke quietly into his PCom as he walked away, the words no longer audible. He paced slowly back and forth, muttering into his PCom for what must have been close to five minutes, and then held a hand above his head. The entire room fell silent immediately.

"Listen up people," he said. "Get those witnesses out of here and prepare for Operation Dishrag."

The witnesses were quickly ushered onto the elevator. Julius watched the doors closing, doing his best to breathe deep and stay calm. No going back now. Linden looked so pale; Julius feared the poor scientist might pass out. Rodriguez's face gave nothing away, but her hands shook. Julius felt his own doing the same.

Some of the technicians produced some sort of weapons—white guns with compact, oval tanks attached to the side.

Linden leaned in and whispered to Julius. "Plasma throwers. Basically flamethrowers, but they throw liquid flame that burns ten times hotter than a conventional flamethrower, and with a relatively small, portable fuel source. Very new tech, very nasty."

The technicians gave the weapons to the agents, and these formed a half circle around the spot directly beneath the vent, from which the ooze monster had dropped down and killed Petyr Franklin. They waited.

The now-silent room had so recently been filled with chatter, with dozens of personnel working independently, that Julius could almost hear the echoes of all that action. Or perhaps he could just hear the wind outside after all, howling with cold rage. He could hear his own heart pounding against his chest for sure. Could hear... something in the vents above.

"Flush it," the leader said into his PCom, and in the dead silence of the room his words boomed and rattled the walls. The agents tensed.

And then there was a hissing sound in the vents, and steaming liquid sluiced through the vent, cascading to the metal floor of the viewing bay. It sloshed past the black-loafered feet of the WalCo agents, who stood still as granite. The moment froze in time—the steam curled slowly from the wet floor, the agents poised, and weapons pointed, the storm churning above the city. And the noise in the vents, louder now. Something squelching and clanging, and it was coming closer. It was coming fast.

With another loud hiss, the ooze monster came catapulting out. It did not fall directly down. It did not parachute. It sped like a bullet out of the vent at an angle that took it directly into contact with the face of one of the plasma-thrower-wielding agents. He dropped his weapon and grabbed at his face and screamed.

The other agents looked at each other, stepped back from their dying comrade, uncertain. Julius tensed, but what could he do?

The technicians began to talk all at once, calling out to the agents with ideas or strategies. A few ran for the elevator, hammering the call button, but another agent stepped between them and the door, trying to keep a quarantine on the room. Surely if the monster got out, it could wreak all kinds of havoc before they had another chance like this.

Out of the mass confusion strode the Immortal. He calmly walked to the nearest agent and took the man's weapon, shouldering him out of the way in the process.

Howls of agony evolved quickly into gargling, wet noises, as acid —no, super-acid Linden had said—poured into the poor man's mouth and dissolved his face. It began to eat its way from the inside out of the man's belly, leaking through the openings between suit buttons. The ooze did not seem to be trying to eat, just to kill. It knew somehow that it needed to defend itself. That it was under attack. Not a mindless creature, then.

The leader pointed his weapon at the still-living agent and fired. A stream of blue-liquid flame struck with such force that dying man and ooze monster alike toppled backwards. The Immortal pressed forward, finger on the trigger, dousing them both with a flame so hot that Julius could feel it from thirty feet away. There was the sound of sizzling, the last strangled scream, and then the other agents joined in, seven more streams of blue heat joining the first. The liquid that had flushed the creature out of the vents evaporated, and steam filled the room. After maybe five seconds of concerted burning, the man stopped, and his lackeys followed suit.

Nothing remained. The metal floor was charred from the heat, and atop it, the biological remnants of man and ooze monster had been reduced to a small pile of ash.

Beside him, Julius' consultant vomited on the floor. Julius himself stood like a statue, his brain refusing to process what he'd seen. Rodriguez whispered something, too soft for Julius to hear. Some curse or prayer.

The leader tossed his weapon on the ground and flicked on his PCom once more. "It's taken care of, sir. Minimal casualties. I'll return for debrief at once."

"Mr. Galloway," one of the technicians said, cautiously approaching the man with the white eyes.

He raised one hand. "Meet me in the elevator." The tech stepped back and slunk into the elevator, clutching some kind of tablet close to his chest.

Galloway. The guy's name was Galloway. Julius had never heard of him but didn't think he'd ever forget the name now.

Galloway strode across the room, and didn't stop until his nose was almost touching Julius'. "Case closed, Special Agent Weaver. My people will clean up our mess—and yours," he said, looking briefly at Linden's expulsion on the floor. "And you can tell your detective friend down below that the threat has passed, and Arc 1 is safe once again."

He stepped past Julius towards the elevator but paused before stepping aboard the car with the cowering technician. "Oh, and Special Agent, if you want to live a long and healthy life, I would recommend that you close this case immediately. It would make me very unhappy to have to come all the way out here to Alaska twice in one year."

With that the man stepped into the elevator, and the doors closed behind him.

"Guess we're waiting for the next one," Julius said, looking at Linden and Rodriguez. Though he tried his best to sound cavalier, he was glad not to have to share an elevator with Galloway. A man who, as far as Julius was concerned, was more monster than the strange ooze that had just been incinerated.

Chapter 11

Three days since "case closed." Three days since Julius had watched an Immortal with a flamethrower take over his case, and in the process of resolving it, burn a man to death in front of a room full of witnesses.

In honor of three days, Julius opened up his third bottle of bourbon. After the first day, he'd given up his shot glass, realizing that it was an unnecessary middleman between the bottle and his mouth. After the second day, he'd given up staying in his quarters, instead drunkenly wandering the slums, and later stopping by the office to have a few drinks with Linden, who was inexplicably lingering despite the fact that his contract had presumably expired.

They'd had very little to say to each other, or at least Julius didn't remember much being said. But then, you drink to forget, not to remember.

On the morning of the third day was when the memo had arrived. Now, Julius pulled it up on his PCom and reread it.

Special Agent Weaver,

Great job seeing the case through to its seizure by WalCo. I was grateful to receive your report on the organism. The

What did it mean? WalCo and other major corporations regularly seized cases from Federal authorities when their own personnel became victims, or when their own private assets were at stake. And in this particular case, they'd already gotten away with it, what did the Director expect Julius to do? What could Julius hope to do?

He looked out the window of his apartment. From here he could see above and across to the west. The Great White Spot roared in full force, winds shredding down old dunes, whirling the white remnants high into the air, and fresh snow falling hard into the mix to build new mountains of powder. The thickness of the snowfall scribed arcane glyphs and elegant patterns in the sky, and the more Julius watched, the more he searched for meaning in them. And in that search found peace. Was it partly the bourbon talking? Maybe. Probably definitely. But he loved his simple and beautiful life here in Nowhere, Alaska. He didn't want to understand what the Director was saying, because the consequences for taking this case any further would be dire.

So, fine. He wouldn't take it any further. He did his job; nobody could say otherwise. And since he wouldn't have another until he retired, he might as well celebrate the re-establishment of his infinite pay-to-work ratio. On a whim, he produced his PCom and dialed Officer Rodriguez's phone number, which he'd received from her three days ago on the pretext that his superiors might want to debrief her on what they'd both seen up in the observation bay that day.

When her face appeared on his screen, she was sweaty, hair tied in a long ponytail. Behind her, a number of men and women in white uniforms were doing some sort of martial arts.

"Is this a bad time, Officer Rodriguez?"

"It's just Sierra now," she said, her face as stoic as always. "I was released by the Arc 1 PD."

"Shit," Julius said. "I'm sorry, I didn't –"

"Don't," she said. "I knew what would happen when I came up with you, but I had to see. Three people died, Special Agent Weaver."

"Well then let me make it up to you, Sierra. Let me buy you dinner tonight."

She paused, and there was a flicker of something in her eyes. What was it? Happiness? Anger? Mirth? "Make it tomorrow night, and we'll give you time to sober up. I prefer my dinner companions not be slurring their words when we talk."

Julius raised his hand to deny his drunkness or as a preface for some witty retort, but then thought better of it. "Fine," he muttered. "I know a great little place, I'll make reservations."

Sierra laughed, musical and strong. "No, I think we'll let the sober person make the reservations. Plus, I've got a craving for French cuisine, and I've got just such a restaurant in mind. I'll text you the details in a bit. See you tomorrow, Julius."

Before he could respond, she disconnected the call. The image of her lingered on his screen for a moment, her smile wide and a little bit mischievous. She'd been laid off because of him, but she didn't seem to care. He did. He was furious that the Arc 1 Police Department would fire her, though he knew it was probably more to do with WalCo than A1PD.

The people of Arc 1 took pride in having their own autonomous police force, but if a corporation like WalCo decided to take over, it would only be a matter of time and money before Arc 1, like all the major cities, was subdivided into corporate security team districts. The only reason it hadn't happened already was that none of the corporations cared much about an obsolete old launch-town that had been eclipsed by half a dozen newer spaceports in the Arctic. If some accountant did a cost-benefit that it would be better to control the place directly and do away with A1PD, that would be the end of the city's autonomy.

He laid down his PCom and took another swig of bourbon. It was starting to burn hard, his body clearly unimpressed with his hard drinking ways. Not like when he was in his twenties, when he could drink anything, and it went down smooth as water. Maybe it was time to put the bottle away and move on. People died, and ooze monsters... well, apparently ooze monsters happened. No reason to stop living.

He hadn't slept much lately, so when his mind decided to shed the weighted blanket of tension he'd been carrying on his shoulders for the last three days, a wave of exhaustion struck him. It had been a trying week, with precious little sleep. He stripped down and crawled into bed immediately. His eyes heavy, he thought of his younger days, passing out after partying all night. Bed was a comfortable place to be, and sleep was good. Maybe tomorrow he would head into the office and see what had become of Dr. Linden. Perhaps the peculiar Nord was sticking around because he was hoping for a more permanent job in the lab. Julius could certainly help arrange it, and the scientist had more than earned the right to stay. He'd be an asset to the other departments with actual caseloads.

That task done, next would come the date. It had been a long time since Julius Weaver had been on a date. It had been a long time since he had... well, best not to think about it unless he wanted his slowly lifting mood to take a heavy death spiral again. It had been a long time, that was all, and he was ready to move on.

Julius smiled and pulled his covers tighter, the fuzz of approaching sleep scrambling his memories with images from his day and with hopes for his tomorrow.

Chapter 12

Julius unfurled slowly from his bed, stretching his creaking joints and rinsing the desiccation of a three-day drinking binge out of his mouth with water from his bathroom faucet. He wasn't old, but he was too old for *this* shit. Drunken detectives and private eyes in old movies always drank without consequences. He tried to rub the hangover out of his eyes, but the light still burned, and his head still throbbed. He wanted to vomit, but he hated vomiting. Hadn't done it in fifteen years and wasn't about to start now.

He pulled the digital display for his bathroom med dispenser. His best friend in the whole world. Tapped a few keys, and a few more, and then a bunch more. Headache, dehydration, nausea, exhaustion. Libido. PTSD. The computer hummed for a moment, the processors juggling symptoms and comparing meds to minimize side effects and ensure that none of the prescribed pills conflicted with one another. After a moment, red words scrolled angrily across the display. "Warning, optimal cocktail has high risk of undesirable side effects." There was a fine-print list beneath the red words, but he didn't bother reading them. He never bothered. Anything really bad, and it wouldn't dispense the meds to begin with. MedCo had enough wrongful death lawsuits without exposing themselves to more for improperly dispensing medication.

He smashed his index finger clumsily at the "Dispense anyway" button, and the little metal tray deployed beneath the display screen. After a friendly beep, five pills came tumbling out, into the palm of his waiting hand. He threw them back, washing them down with more sink water. It would take a few minutes for them to kick in, but by the time he was at the office, he'd be as good as new, his terrible hangover a lesson already forgot.

The walk to the office proved uneventful. He took the tubes, a few shortcuts through some office buildings, the fastest route to work. He wanted to speak with Linden early. He suspected he had an apology to make, and he definitely wanted to get working on finding Linden a permanent position in the Agency, if that's what the scientist's angle was. Above, yesterday's blizzard howled even harder, the sky little more than a wall of white.

When Julius arrived, Linden waited eagerly in their mutual office. The frumpy Nordic scientist rose to his feet with a wide grin. "I have more information. Have you considered what I told you the other day?"

"Huh?" Julius said.

"You *do* remember what I told you the other day?"

Julius groaned. "Linden, you know I was drunk when we spoke last, right? *Drunk*, drunk. Hammered. Are you a drinker?"

"I have an Aquavit occasionally, but" he trailed off, confusion plain across his face.

"Blackout drunk, man. I don't remember a thing you told me; you'll have to start over."

"Oh, fine, no problem," Linden said. "Well, first of all, I was going back over the ooze monster residue that we got from the snow, and I found something... illuminating."

"No, no, no," Julius said. "That case is closed. Are you crazy, going up against a fixer like that with the backing of an enormous corporation like WalCo?"

"He's rather intimidating, I admit, but I'm still on retainer. The Director is paying me extra to keep looking into the matter. I figured it'd be safe. I mean, you're the FBINA after all, aren't you?"

Could the scientist really be this dense? Julius could hardly believe it, but he found his heart racing at the prospect of carrying things further. What could the Director be doing, going after WalCo like this? With a little team in Alaska, of all places?

"Special Agent Weaver?" Linden said. "Are you okay?"

Julius shook his head. "No, I'm not okay. I don't want to know a thing about ooze monsters or WalCo or anything. That man, the leader of that horror show in the viewing bay, he's age stasis, Linden. I know you know what that means. He's an Immortal. Do you know the kind of money you need for that procedure? Of course you don't. People like you and I aren't even rich enough to know how rich you have to be for a procedure like that. But it's the kind of money that buys immunity from everything you've ever done. The kind of money that turns your vaguest desire into reality. I don't want to die for this."

He paused. The scientist opened his mouth to speak, but Julius cut him off. "Anyway, everyone's dead, Linden. It's not even a missing person's case anymore. Nobody missing, not my problem. Case closed."

"But the Director," Linden pleaded.

"The Director can go to hell," Julius said. His breath was getting shallow. Was this a panic attack, or one of those undesirable side effects? His lungs ached from a shortage of oxygen. The walls were closing in. He needed to get out, and fast. "I need some air," Julius wheezed, stepping out of the office and into the elevator.

May Ellis rose from her desk as he stumbled past. "Julius, are you okay?" she asked. He could not look at her, waved vaguely in her direction, pushing his way through the too-thick air towards the elevator. Inside, he hammered at the R button until the doors slid shut.

The ride to the roof seemed to take hours, a ponderous trip through Titan's thick atmosphere, his spacesuit breather cracked, his last bits of oxygen slipping out. He saw his parents in the distance, standing outside a colony hab module wrapped on all sides by a white picket fence. His father held a pitchfork and they both waved at him, the movements clumsy with the bulk of their spacesuits. He reached for them—surely, they would help him, surely if he could just get to them and get inside then he could breathe normally again. But they faded and he found himself just standing in the elevator, the whooshing hydraulics the only sound in the world.

When the doors opened onto the rooftop garden, he stepped out, gulping down air with greed. Not that Arc air was any different outside a building as inside one, but still, out here he could finally begin to breathe again. The silent roaring of the blizzard outside the bubble, the hidden patterns scribed by the whip and lash of white calmed him, gradually bringing his rapidly beating heart to a more manageable speed, returning regular breathing patterns to his chest.

He closed his eyes and then opened them. He'd had enough of ooze monsters and Immortals for one career. Special Agent Julius Weaver wouldn't have anything to do with any of that from here on out. Maybe today he would take another personal day. Tomorrow, he'd politely inform the Director that the case was closed, and that was it, he would return to work. Hopefully. And hey, Marcus could probably get him work if the Director fired him. His old partner was always angling to hire him, and maybe it was finally time for Julius Weaver to sell out.

But all of that was for another day. A day called "tomorrow." Today, Julius would spend some time on the roof, and then he would go home and get ready. He had a date, after all.

CHAPTER 13

"What do you mean, 'this isn't a date?'" Julius asked.

"I mean," Sierra said, mumbling around a mouthful of duck confit, "that you got me fired and I really had a craving for this place."

Julius sat back heavily in his chair. It was a nice place. Small tables, spaced far apart, ornate bistro style chairs. Kitschy French movie posters from the early 21st century adorned the walls, and servers in ties made frequent stops at diners' tables to serve bread and refill wine glasses.

Sierra gestured to the server, and he immediately arrived to refill her wine, which was empty already even though they'd only just received their appetizer. Julius waved him off, taking another sip of water from his own glass. No wine, no more whiskey, no more booze ever. Or at least not until his liver recovered from his last binge.

"So, you don't have any interest in me at all? I thought we shared a moment, working on that case."

She chased down another mouthful of food with a big swig of a red wine with a long French name. "I find that the French provinces still produce the best wine in the world," she said. "Wouldn't you agree?"

He swiped his hand through the holo display in the middle of the table, pulling up the wine list once more. Read through the names. Lots of French words. The only one he really recognized was "chateau," which was featured prominently in many of the listings. "I'm more of a whiskey man," he said.

She looked over her wine glass at him, before setting it down and leaning forward. "Listen, Special Agent Weaver. I don't play for your team. Or rather, I *do* play for your team."

"Ah," Julius said, warmth rising to his face. "You also prefer the company of women. I'm usually better at discerning that." He paused. "So, you allowed me to blunder around in my ignorance because you wanted a free meal? That seems pretty cold."

She leaned back in her chair. "Not really, no. I actually planned to try and convince you to let me in on the investigation, even though I'm not A1PD anymore. I thought I might wait until you'd had your fill of the most amazing Coq au Vin in Alaska to ask, but you really get right to the heart of things."

"What investigation?" Julius asked.

She cocked her head to the side. "The same one we've been working on? You know, impossible ooze monster eats people, gets incinerated by corporate goon? Seemed pretty memorable to me."

Julius breathed deeply and slowly. Didn't want to let the room close in on him again, didn't want to panic again. Just calmly address the issue and move on. "No, no, it's closed already. There's nothing left to investigate, no case to let you in on, sorry," he said.

"Julius, I thought for sure you'd keep investigating when you found out that these deaths were homicide, rather than collateral damage from some out-of-control experiment."

"What do you mean, homicide?" Julius said.

"Did you not speak to Dr. Linden? He told me he'd informed you."

Julius groaned, his hands on his temples. "He tried. He did, but I was drunk. He tried again when I was sober, I think, but I didn't want to hear it. Don't you two understand what we're up against here? What could happen to us?"

"I'm not an idiot. And neither is Linden. We both know what we're up against. I already gave up my job following this thing, and now we have solid evidence that those deaths were pre-meditated..." she took another swig of wine—a long one, draining the glass.

The silence expanded between them as Julius felt the comfort of his life orbiting away from him. He had to know what made them so sure it was homicide. But once he knew, that would be it. Assuming the evidence measured up, it would be impossible for him to let it go. He simply wasn't built that way. Corporations like WalCo regularly got away with murder, it was true. Yet the idea of them getting away with it because he, Julius, was afraid to pursue the case to its end—he couldn't live with that.

All of which meant that Julius was about to get sucked into a David and Goliath battle between the slowly dying FBINA and corporate behemoth WalCo. A losing fight, a foregone conclusion. But then, Julius had already chosen years of obsolescence over a fat paycheck safe in the corporate womb at BioMart or elsewhere. So that was it then. He sighed. By this time tomorrow, in all likelihood, he would be well on his way to an early death, or permanent incarceration in an off-books corporate holding facility.

The waiter arrived with steaming hot plates of something that looked delicious. He barely noticed. He was staring at Sierra, and she was staring back, and the server said something and they didn't respond so he walked away, and well, fuck it. "Okay," Julius said. "What's this thing that Dr. Linden discovered that you two insist means its homicide?"

Sierra waved the server back over, to refill her wine again. "Something about nanobots," she said, digging into her food. "Basically, the ooze monster was being remotely controlled when it killed those people. I'll let the good doctor fill you in on the details, it was all a bit too technical for me."

"Remote controlled ooze monster? Shit. Okay, I guess I do need details. He's probably still moping around in my office," Julius said. "Where does Hallis stand in all this?"

"Nowhere. He got laid off too," she said between bites.

"Shit, really? He didn't even go up with us."

She took another long drink of her wine and set the glass down, staring at Julius. After an uncomfortably long pause she finally spoke. "It's WalCo. What did you really expect when you forced your way past those goons? At least, due to his age, they had to give him his pension. But you better believe he loses it if he gets involved in anything, so we are *not* bringing him back in. Clear?"

"Clear," Julius said, picking idly at his food, lost in thought.

CHAPTER 14

The first hint was a faint scratching in the vents above that connected the air filtration system for the restaurant with the Arc's primary ventilation system. Not that you wouldn't expect the occasional creak or errant noise from the infrastructure of an old city like Arc 1, but Julius went into high alert mode the moment he mentally committed to picking up this case. The noise tickled the hairs on the back of his neck, and he made a point to pay attention to those feelings. The subconscious was much smarter than the conscious mind, better at connecting dots. Not to be lightly ignored.

Sierra was investigating the dessert menu when he heard the noise, and she didn't seem to notice. She said something, gesturing at the menu, but Julius had already tuned out the everyday world. The rich smells of French cuisine, the happy chatter of dining patrons, whatever Sierra was saying. It all blurred into a flat background. His senses all strained towards one purpose—the discernment of danger. He heard the noise again, and then a few seconds later, a commotion in the kitchen. Shattered glass, a cry of surprise. Nothing terribly out of place, but enough for Sierra to look up at Julius and, seeing his expression, turn towards the kitchen herself.

Then they both saw it. A small black blob scaling the far wall just above the door to the kitchen. It was on the ceiling in barely a second. Julius's brain and body diverged. His body rose, sidearm suddenly in hand, firing at the monster. With the soft whispered hush of the handgun's magnetic delivery system, several tungsten-uranium pellets struck the creature at staggeringly high velocity. Each impact spattered the ceiling with the viscous liquid that seemed to comprise the creature's body, but it continued—directly towards him, past numerous other potential food sources—unabated. When it drew near, it seemed to leap from the ceiling, propelling itself directly towards his face. Only narrowly was he able to dive clear, rolling to his knees to watch the creature impact the far wall, and immediately begin again to move towards him.

His body on automatic after years of combat training, Julius's brain churned rapidly through the facts:

One. Should the creature touch him at all, he suspected, what Linden had referred to as a super-acid would sear through his flesh. He did not like his odds even with the hyperdense muscle and carbon-nanotube bones in his bio-auged arms.

Two. It was bypassing the civilians around him, and therefore seemed to be targeting him specifically, which meant that A) he didn't need to worry about civilian collateral, and B) there was a higher intelligence at work. He filed that away for later and moved on.

Three. Heat. Linden had said that the cold provided the best conductivity for the creature to pass electrical currents over its body, and blah blah blah. The Immortal had killed the creature with a flamethrower. Heat was his friend. Where do you find heat in a restaurant? The kitchen.

Julius rose from his knees, holstering his weapon as he did, and sprinted towards the kitchen. Sierra was a few steps ahead of him, already halfway there and gesturing frantically for him to follow. How the hell was she running faster than him in that cocktail dress? He barely had time to wonder. He could hear the creature's movement, a weird combination of soft static and a sort of wet spattering like water dripping sideways. The sound was getting closer.

He grabbed an empty table for four, his arm muscles straining against his skin, and spun around mid-stride to heave it at the creature. It splattered against the flat wood of the table, and Julius spun back around to finish his sprint to the kitchen. Behind him, a hiss of synth-wood dissolving, and when he looked over his shoulder again, the creature had already burned through the table. He'd barely slowed it down, bought himself maybe a second.

But a second was all he needed. He burst into the kitchen a few steps behind Sierra, smashing through the swinging doors without slowing. Panicked staff were already in the process of fleeing out the back door, having been the first to see the ooze monster. Sierra stood there; a huge metal pot full of something steaming in her hands. The ooze monster was on his heels, he was blocking her line of sight; he hit the ground, sliding past her feet first as she upended the boiling contents of her pot. Broken glass dug into his legs as he slid and something scalding singed the back of his neck as Sierra poured, but then he was back on his feet, he and Sierra backing away from the ooze monster.

It moved slower now, but still it came. They pulled more hot food from the burners, hitting the creature over and over again with hot liquids, hot solids, hot anything. They poured steaming gourmet French cuisine onto the creature until it stopped moving forward, and instead began merely to twitch in place.

Julius looked around, but in a heartbeat, the creature began crawling forward again. Sierra hit it with another pot of soup, but they were running out of hot food. There was a second pause, the creature twitching again, and this time Julius made good use of his time. He grabbed a huge cast iron pot with a great big cast iron lid, and scooped the ooze monster in. The lid on top, he slammed it down on one of the burners, cranking it to its highest setting. He held the lid down, but there was no activity from within, nothing trying to get out. After several minutes, he stepped back.

For a time, Julius and Sierra simply watched the pot, the cooking goo monster, afraid to look inside. Eventually, he heard police sirens. No chance of getting Hallis, if they'd retired him already, so one of the other detectives would be inside shortly, and Julius couldn't have that. He trusted some of A1PD, but not all of them. Not with WalCo money on the line. And anyway, someone was trying to kill him. Five minutes after he all but agreed to continue looking into the case, and a second goo monster squirts past fifteen other diners, making a beeline for him—that was no coincidence. Best not to get anyone else involved who wasn't already.

"The police," Sierra started, but he cut her off with a motion from his hand. Held his finger to his mouth. *Shh.* Understanding in her eyes, right away. Good. He grabbed the pot. Time to go. Hopefully the monster was dead, or at least incapacitated for long enough to be brought into the FBI lab, for Linden to take a look. The cast iron would hold its heat for a time. If they hurried, they would make it back to the lab. If not... well, best not to think about that.

At the back exit from the restaurant, Julius paused at the door. Sierra had not followed. His heart rate rose. Was she selling him out to her former co-workers? Going rogue? Where had she gone? His questions were quickly put to rest when she appeared from around the corner with a hand-torch and a can of spray-oil. Perfect. If the creature got loose, they'd stand a chance at putting it down after all.

"Back to the FBI lab," he mouthed to her, and then they were out the door. A captured goo monster, a huge leap forward in solving this mad case, the case that would probably end up killing them both in the end. But that didn't matter anymore. WalCo had inadvertently locked him into the case for good. He tended to take it personally when someone tried to kill him, and anyway they had proven to him that the creature wasn't just a mindless synthetic animal eating to survive. It was a custom-made attack dog, trained or controlled for specific and nefarious purposes.

CHAPTER 15

What a pair they must have made, Sierra in her cocktail dress holding a can of spray oil and a lighter at ready; and Julius in his suit, the fabric torn and his blood seeping through in the legs, holding a closed cast iron pot like so much roadkill. Security on the ground floor didn't say anything—they knew Julius—but the looks on their faces spoke volumes. When the two burst into the lab, the techs mostly didn't bother to look up. That is, until Julius shouted for someone to page Dr. Linden ASAP. At 8 pm, could the good doctor still be in the building? Fortunately, he was.

Julius left Sierra and the ooze monster confit in the lab to explain things to Linden, and took a turn down a few lesser used hallways, to find himself in the debugging office. He was grateful she had understood that Julius must have been bugged back in the observation bay. But how? He'd never let Galloway touch him during that whole horror show, and anyway, his clothes were different now.

Sitting behind the desk in the debugging office was a bored looking, bespectacled young man—face still pimply. He was watching some stream on a little holo-projection from his PCom. When he looked up, he seemed surprised to see someone in his office.

Before Julius could speak, the young man, whose nameplate identified him as "Agent Reid," gestured at an electro-pad in the center of the desk in front of him. Julius swiped his finger across it, formulating his situation in words that popped up on a sister display that the young agent could read.

Was bugged by someone who never actually touched me,

Before Julius could finish, Agent Reid nodded sagely and rose quickly to his feet with a small wand in his hand. He punched in a few buttons and then waved it around Julius's clothing. When that received no result, he expanded the search to hands and feet, and then finally to Julius's head. When the young agent passed the wand across Julius's eyes, there was a crackle, and tiny sparks in Julius's vision, from where his eyes met his nose on both sides. He recoiled, though the experience wasn't painful.

"Wow," Reid said. "You must have pissed off someone really powerful. That is some expensive nanotech right there."

"Care to elaborate? I haven't kept up on the latest surveillance nanos," Julius said.

The young man furrowed his eyebrows. "Which department are you in?"

"Special Agent Julius Weaver in Missing Persons."

"Ah, well that explains why you haven't kept up with the trends. But not who the hell would care enough to invest this kind of tech in bugging you...." Reid sort of trailed off, muttering speculations to himself.

Julius was used to this sort of thing, working in his department. But he didn't have nearly enough time to deal with it today. "Listen up kid, I have some serious shit going down in the lab that I need to get back to. I need you to tell me everything you can about this tech, and I need you to do it quickly. Can you manage that?"

Reid looked up as though surprised to see Julius still there. "Right, sorry Special Agent Weaver. So basically, what you have is a handful of nanobots with autonomous flight capability. Micro-drones. Too small to be seen, but they were guided remotely by someone who landed them on you. From there, they travel up to your eyes, where they take in light and can provide an accurate facsimile of what you're looking at. Probably had about a dozen on you working in conjunction to see what you were seeing and hear what you were hearing."

Julius rubbed his fingers into the places where there had supposedly been listening devices implanted. Couldn't feel a thing, but he knew they'd been there. Probably still were attached to his skin, only coming off as his enormous fingers wiped the tiny dead flakes of them away. "Who has this tech?"

Reid shrugged. "SecuriGroup has a patent, but that doesn't mean most of the megacorps haven't already stolen it for private use."

"Okay, thanks, Agent. You've been very helpful."

"Good luck, Special Agent Weaver. I have a feeling you're going to need it," Reid said.

Julius paused at the threshold. He'd deduced that he was bugged on account of the fact that the attack had only come after Sierra persuaded him to take another look into the case. Linden and she had been showing interest for days but were unscathed. It made sense, then, that Julius—the only member of the little team with the clout to drive a real investigation—had become the focus of these surveillance efforts. But it was probably better safe than sorry.

"Hey Reid, can you come with me and scan my partners with that wand as well?"

#

Ten minutes later, Julius was back in the lab. Sierra was looking flabbergasted, and Linden was laughing hysterically. The lab techs had all given up their work and stood gawking at the cast iron pot.

Julius gestured at Linden and Sierra, and Reid gave them the wand treatment. Linden looked at him quizzically, still chuckling, but Sierra already knew a suspected bug was in play. Reid blushed as he ran the wand along Sierra's curves, his pimples blending into the red rising to his cheeks. Sparks crackled in both Sierra's and Linden's eyes as well. Somebody was taking no chances. Somebody with great wealth. Almost certainly WalCo's Immortal fixer. Galloway.

"Thanks," Julius said to Reid, before turning to Linden. "Shouldn't you be setting up some kind of goo monster containment system?"

"Seriously, why are you laughing?" Sierra asked.

"I'm sorry," Linden said, wiping at his eyes where the nanobots had sparked. "But what was that?"

"Nano-drone surveillance apparently. We were bugged, guessing by WalCo when we were in the viewing room."

"Ah," Linden nodded. "It's safe now?"

"It's safe," Sierra chimed in. "Now tell us what the hell is so funny?"

"It's just that the two of you accidentally set up the perfect containment system for this thing. That cast iron pot is a natural Faraday Cage."

"A Faraday Cage? What does insulating the ooze monster against external signals have to do with anything?" Sierra asked.

Julius wasn't following, but that was okay, eventually things would become clear. If Linden said an iron pot was the perfect containment for the creature, then that was good enough for him. It certainly hadn't shown any signs of life since they'd put it inside. He relaxed for the first time in hours, grabbing a nearby stool and sitting. His legs throbbed, oozing blood around embedded shards of glass.

"Well," Linden said, adjusting the pot to sit more firmly on the table, "as I told you both on separate occasions, these ooze monsters aren't really monsters at all. They're sort of organic-electronic composites. And they aren't autonomous at all, there is nothing that serves the purpose of a central nervous system. I couldn't figure it out, until, well, I did."

"What are you saying?" Julius asked. "How do they function without some kind of brain?"

Linden began to talk with his hands, growing more animated the more he was asked to explain things. "That's the beauty of these units, they're actually accessed remotely. Nano-machines seeded throughout the organic matter allow an external signal to be transmitted that is translated at the local level to various actions."

"And that's why the cast iron pot is the perfect way to hold the thing, no signal will reach the ooze monster to reactivate it, because the iron pot is a natural Faraday Cage," Sierra finished.

"That's the second time in the past fifteen minutes that someone has mentioned remote-controlled nanobots. Are you telling me someone was piloting this ooze monster from a computer somewhere?" Julius knew the answer as he asked it. That's exactly what Linden was saying, and that's why they were telling him these killings were homicide. But what was the motive?

They'd need to investigate the victims again, figure out why WalCo would want them dead. Linden was saying something, but Julius was already in his own head plotting their next three moves. So much to do, and they'd have to be stealthy, couldn't give away the game. The enemy knew everything he knew thus far. Knew what Linden knew before Julius did, because they'd been watching him talk to Linden when he'd been too drunk to take it all in. Had been watching Linden work. Eavesdropping on whatever conversations Linden and Sierra had had.

"Julius?" Sierra said.

He looked up. "Yes, sorry, what?"

"What now?"

"Now my legs hurt, so we're going to go up to my office and I'm going to pick out little pieces of glass while we figure out our next course of action. Dr. Linden, can you possibly trace the source of the signal, get us a location?"

Linden seemed to consider for a moment. "Yes, I suppose I can. I'll need some help from some of these gentlemen in the lab, though; we'll need to set up a larger Faraday Cage, one that we can open and close, as it were. We'll let little bursts of signal through—not enough for the creature to fully reactivate, but enough to trace the signal to its source, I think."

"Good. Use whoever you need, and I'm going to post a couple of security personnel at the entrance to the lab here, as I'm not sure WalCo won't attack the office directly. Let me know when you make some progress."

Some of the techs protested being co-opted, but he shut them down quickly. The Director wanted this; the Director could clean up his mess. He was through tiptoeing around; he was through with people trying to kill him. He was going to find the people responsible for this monstrosity and these murders and he was going to take them down.

He stopped at the door on his way out the lab and turned back. Linden was already rallying his support staff to his side, explaining something very technical. "Dr. Linden?" Julius said.

"Hmm?" he looked up.

"You made it through this whole procedure without undermining yourself. It's nice to see you picking up a little confidence. Keep it up."

Linden blushed, waved Julius off, turning back to his fellow technicians and diving into his work.

CHAPTER 16

When Julius and Sierra emerged from the elevator en route to his office, May Ellis rose immediately from her desk at the sight of the two of them. Did she ever sleep, he wondered? Shouldn't the Discontent Unit have a night secretary to keep up with their heavy workload?

"My goodness, Julius, what happened to you? Who's this? What's going *on*?"

"May, this is Sierra Rodriguez, ex-A1PD. She's consulting with me on my case. As for the rest of it, well if I told you, you wouldn't believe me and I'd be putting you in danger to boot. If you'll excuse us, we need to get to work."

"I most certainly will not excuse you," she said. "You're injured and you need medical attention. You don't have to tell me what's going on, but I'm not going to just let you bleed all over the carpet. Breeze past me into your office if you like, but I'm coming in with my first aid kit."

Julius shrugged, and the three of them entered his office together, May Ellis with first aid kit in hand. Sierra sat quietly in Linden's chair. Julius sat on his desk, feet on the visitor's chair, and watched as May Ellis went to town. She cut away the torn pant legs with some tiny scissors, and then sprayed the whole area down with an anti-bacterial foam. It crackled and evaporated quickly in the air, but it continued to burn like hell on all the tiny lacerations in his legs.

And then she got out the tweezers. Minutes felt like hours as she extracted shards of broken glass from deep within his flesh. The blood flowed freely, and he gritted his teeth, until at last she had a pile of glass shards at her feet. She wiped his legs clean and looked them over for any pieces she'd missed. Apparently finding none, she sprayed his legs with the anti-bacterial foam again, and then followed it up with a plastic clotting spray that quickly filled in the holes in his legs and dried up, rapidly stopping the blood flow.

"Okay," she rose. "Probably should have had a medic do that, but nobody's on duty in the building at night, and it was clear you weren't going to a hospital."

"That was impressive," Sierra said. "Do you have experience as a medic or EMT or something?"

"Nope," May said, gathering up the broken glass and placing it all gently in the nearby trash bin. "Just took some first aid classes online; figured it might come in handy, and it sure did."

"Well, thanks very much for patching me up." Julius rose and walked around his desk to take his usual seat.

"Now you listen up. You lost a lot of blood so take it easy tonight, okay?"

"Yes ma'am," Julius smiled. She returned his smile with a stern look, and then stepped out of his office to return to her own desk.

When she was gone, Sierra rose, closed the door behind her, and dragged Linden's chair into the space across from Julius, shoving aside the now-bloody visitor's chair. She sat down and leaned in, practically whispering, "Julius Weaver, what on Earth are you doing trying to date me when you're across the hall from *her*?"

"May Ellis?" Julius said absently, plugging his PCom into his holo-disk, and booting the system up.

"Hell yes, May Ellis. She's dainty and strong and redheads that sexy do *not* come along every day and hot damn, but does she ever have a thing for you."

"I suppose I never pay much attention to my co-workers here. I've been kind of a recluse these last three years, what with not having a single case and all. You really think she has a thing for me?"

"If we survive this case, you had better make a move, or so help me I'll do it for you," Sierra said.

"Fair enough," Julius said. When he thought about it, he *had* noticed her from time to time. He'd always thought of her as just a quiet secretary, but Sierra was right: They'd seen a fiery side of May Ellis tonight. He liked it. He liked it a lot, in fact, but he didn't have time for it just now, so he put it out of his mind.

The display booted, and Julius swiped through various department files with ease—he was adept at navigating the FBI bureaucracy—until he had the one he wanted. Sierra watched, evidently content to wait. He punched in information as fast as he could, occasionally asking her for bits of her personal information. She gave these unflinchingly.

"There," he said, swiping away the final screen triumphantly. "Sierra Rodriguez is officially an FBI consultant. Now you and Linden have authority to act with me on this case. Also, you will get paid if we don't die."

"Thank you," she said. "Now I can buy my own dinner again. If we don't die."

He grinned. "So, let's talk next steps. Assuming Dr. Linden successfully traces the signal on that ooze monster, we will probably find ourselves trying to arrest personnel inside a private WalCo facility."

"Do we even have authority to do that?" Sierra asked.

"That depends on which legal scholar you ask. Most of the stuff that the megacorps do was only signed into law by the Global Charter. Technically, the North American Federal Government has laws on the books that would allow us to arrest anyone on the continent. But the question isn't authority, it's power. No megacorp is going to acknowledge any North American Federal laws. If they have armed security, we're going to have a shoot-out on our hands. And even given that, even assuming we make an arrest, we'll never get them on anything in a court of law unless we happen to run into a judge that they can't buy. And most of those are already dead."

"So really the best we can do is haul someone in, make a public trial of it, and hope that the negative public opinion impacts their profits enough that we can call it 'justice.'" Sierra said.

"Mostly, yes," Julius said. "And then WalCo would throw enough money around to blacklist us from any future employment options. If we're lucky. If we're unlucky, they would just put out a corporate warrant for our deaths, and we'd be toast. But I wouldn't have agreed to this if I didn't think there was more to it. The Director of the FBINA has been following this personally, and I'm pretty sure he has some kind of agenda. I'm counting on him to make something out of this if we can get an arrest and enough evidence. I'm counting on him to have our backs afterwards."

"So, we go in with bodycams, do our best to arrest the responsible parties, and leave it in his hands?"

"Yep."

There was silence at that. It seemed like a bleak prospect. Hope to maybe find the people transmitting to the ooze monster, bust in and duke it out with private security that probably outnumbered and outgunned them, find "some evidence," and bring home an arrest (arrest who?); all of this so that the Director could possibly make some charges stick and somehow protect them with a secret legal strategy that he might or might not have. Julius was having second thoughts. Or to be more accurate, third thoughts, as he'd never really gotten over his initial misgivings.

"Three people are dead, Special Agent. I can see it on your face, but you can't give up now. And anyway, now that the bug is fried, they wouldn't know you'd given up and they'd come after us all anyway. Our only choice is to see this through to the end. Do you want to be running from ooze monsters your whole life?"

Sierra was right. He knew she was right. He pulled up a database of WalCo research facilities, thought he might have a go at narrowing down the field in case Linden came up blank on the signal. He had a moment to survey the field, but before he could dive in, there were alarms. Red-light-flashing alarms, blaring klaxons. He knew what it meant, even if he'd never heard them before. Someone was attacking the building.

"The lab," Sierra said, rising to her feet alongside Julius.

He reached into the back of his top drawer, grabbed his spare sidearm, and tossed it to Sierra. Same drawer, other side of the desk, the weapon's magazine, tossed that to her too. She locked and loaded, and they were out into the hall and on the way to the elevator with weapons ready before the start of the panicked page from the security office.

"The building is under attack by unknown assailants. They've cleared the entrance and are currently moving towards the 7th floor. All armed personnel are instructed to move to the 7th floor and assist."

"Lock yourself in my office," Julius shouted at May Ellis as they sprinted past her to the elevator. Down the elevator and halfway to the lab was when they saw the first body. One of the CSIs, who'd clearly been unarmed, sprawled face-down over a pile of bloody storage discs. These guys weren't taking prisoners. WalCo must be really desperate.

Julius rounded the corner to the lab, Sierra right behind him, and there were the two security personnel, dead, bullet holes in their vests, which could only mean gauss weapons. There was a man in a black tactical suit, black mask, black recon hood, and a compact submachine gun in hand. Heavily augmented but with no identifiable corporate markers. WalCo black ops. Highly trained and deadly. He opened up on Julius and Sierra immediately.

Julius barely had time to duck back around the corner, tackling Sierra to the ground. The high-velocity magnetic slugs from the gauss weapon punched holes through the wall directly over their heads, peppering the far wall and showering them in white plaster dust.

Two could play at that game. Where would the assailant be now? Would he be approaching slowly, to confirm the kill? No, he was corporate, and he'd been ordered to guard the door. He'd be locked directly in place, following his orders to the letter.

Julius rose to a crouch, and pointed his sidearm at the wall, lining it up with his memory of where the attacker had been standing, and squeezed the trigger six times in quick succession. Six magnetized flechettes coughed out with a whisper, punched through the wall with a soft crinkle. Julius heard a grunt and a thump; when he and Sierra rounded the corner again, there were three bodies instead of two.

They moved together, Julius on point, into the lab's lobby. The secretary had been gunned down, and one of the techs was dead on the far side of the room. Sierra and he cleared the room, or so he thought until he saw motion at the peripheral of his vision.

One of the assailants rose from hiding behind the secretary's desk, he had gotten the drop on them, they were both dead. Except they weren't. As soon as he popped up, Sierra's gun coughed three times, and the gunman fell over dead, three holes clustered tightly, center mass. They might just make it through this after all.

Then they heard it. Screams. *Agonized* screams. The sound of bones crunching. They stopped short—that was the sound of an ooze monster feeding, it could be nothing else. The creature was loose, reactivated. Julius was torn—they had to get Linden out, but there wasn't anything here to fight the ooze monster with. Maybe there was some kind of fire starter in the lab, but that thing moved so fast, could they really hope to capture it again?

Sierra met his inaction with action, plunging forward. He followed. No plan, then, but he couldn't let her go alone.

They followed more screams deeper into the lab. Apparently, Linden had moved the ooze monster from the primary laboratory area, further into the depths of the facility. No more dead bodies here, he must've conscripted most of the night techs to help him. The screams led them to the bio-research wing of the facility. Sierra threw open the door, and the two of them moved in.

There was the ooze monster, directly in front of them. Blood spatter pooled around it; two more submachine guns, half-liquefied, rested nearby. The thing didn't move towards them, it simply quivered in place for a moment, before sliding quickly along the metal floor and up into an opening in a largish, metal box that looked to have at one point been used for handling bio-agents. Linden stepped around the box, PCom in hand, and shut the box behind the ooze monster.

"Did you –" Sierra started.

"All clear," the voice over the comms announced. "The building is clear of hostiles."

A number of lab techs emerged from a storage room nearby at the announcement, and upon seeing Linden standing near the bloody remnants of the attackers, gave out a hearty cheer.

"What the hell just happened?" Julius asked.

"I hacked the ooze monster's signal, used it to kill those ruffians," Linden said.

"You can *do* that?" Sierra asked.

"Apparently," Linden shrugged. "I didn't have a weapon, and I'd just finished deciphering the signal when we were attacked. It was a lucky longshot, and I put everyone in danger. I'm very sorry."

"Are you kidding me? That's amazing," Julius said. "I couldn't think of a more poetic way of killing WalCo thugs that had the gall to attack the FBI offices."

"So, you decoded the signal and hacked the ooze monster?" Sierra asked. "I would think it would be harder to just hack a high-tech WalCo experimental weapon like that. Like, a lot harder."

"You would indeed, but it seems they had their hands full. Someone else was trying to gain access the whole time," Linden said.

"So," Julius said slowly, "It's not out of the question that the first one was also hacked when it killed that WalCo employee, turning what might have been a weapons test on the dregs of society into a high-profile public murder. A retaliation of some sort, perhaps?"

"Then this could really be two cases?" Sierra said.

"Indeed," Linden said.

"Well for now, let's focus on what we know for sure. Dr. Linden, were you able to track the signal before you took over?" Julius asked.

Linden looked down at his PCom, fiddled with a few commands, and then the holo-projector displayed a map of Alaska. There was a blip in the very far northern reaches, about two hundred kilometers from Arc 1.

"I'm pretty sure there's no on-books facility at that location," Sierra said.

There wasn't—Julius remembered the list and there was nothing in Alaska at all.

"A WalCo secret research facility hidden in the Alaskan wilderness? We know where we're going next," Julius said. "We'll worry about the other hacker later; we need to take the fight to WalCo first. They made this thing, and they attacked us in our own office, killing at least six FBI personnel. They're going to pay dearly."

CHAPTER 17

Two hours into the cleanup, Julius got a call he would never have expected.

Most of the FBINA offices were running on automatic. Half in shock but soldiering on. People had lost close friends and co-workers, but everyone wanted to work to nail the responsible party. To take care of the dead. Julius generally kept to himself, aside from May Ellis from time to time, but folks—especially the lab and security folks—formed a tightly-knit community. It took a certain kind of person to go into Federal law enforcement in an era when corporations ruled the world.

There were no identifying markers on the assailants, but already the lab techs had begun tagging the dead corp-soldiers in facial-recog searches. Several had popped up as security consultants for subsidiaries of WalCo. Could you prove they were a WalCo hit squad in a court of law? Only if you had a judge that didn't care about money, threats to his or her own life, and being gainfully employed. Palpable frustration cloyed the air.

Julius was dragging a body when his PCom rang. He set it down gently and answered the call. Luther Fisk's face materialized in the air, the little holo-engine whirring to render the details. There was no platinum grin this time. The man grimaced—blood running in rivulets down the left side of his face. It seemed he was missing an ear.

"I got to digging after you and I spoke, Agent Weaver. Couldn't have someone on my turf holding tech to fool gene hounds without sharing it. I didn't find much of anything, but I guess I got close enough to something or someone. There's a black ops team hitting my place right now. Shot my damn ear off. I need backup—happy to share what I learned and help you take down whatever sons of bitches are hitting my place. Get over here, yesterday, and I may just be alive to tell you what I know."

After he spoke, Luther lifted a weapon—an old automatic rifle called a Kalashnikov—and severed the connection.

CHAPTER 18

It hadn't taken Julius long to grab Sierra and a team from Vice that would want to be included in anything going down at the Speak Easy. But by the time they arrived on the scene, it was all over.

The streets of the Entertainment District were empty this time around. The only sound came from holo ads flickering in the distance—the soft mutter of commerce. A hundred algorithms offering a hundred deals of the century to blank stone and dark windows. These were silenced as the agents charged past, badges muting everything within range.

Inside the Speak Easy was a blood bath. The bouncer at the door—the same one from when Julius came by—lay spread-eagled on his back at the entrance, a gaping bloody hole in the center of his forehead. Poor bastard probably never saw it coming. Too slow to react if he did.

Julius and the team walked past smooth bullet holes where neon light shone through from the outside. Their boots squelched in thick pools of blood at the entrance. Julius saw no bodies, but based on the quantity of blood, at least four or five had been killed here. The acrid scent of bleach mixed in with the iron tang of the blood on the floor, an overpowering miasma that sent two of the agents retching into the corner—no bodies and no DNA evidence. This crew had been quite a bit more careful than the one that hit the FBI offices. Though perhaps that level of care was just the purview of the victor.

A shattered turret dangled halfway out of a recessed wall panel near the entrance. It had been heavy-duty, too, reinforced carbon-nano-tube joints, heavy-duty alloy components. It took a lot of firepower to take that thing out.

Past the entrance and the destroyed turret, there *were* bodies. Lots of bodies. The WalCo black ops team had come in spraying. Bullet holes and blood spatter made a retro-modern mosaic of the far wall. The faux-wood bars on either side of the room had been chewed to shreds. Almost a dozen patrons lay where they fell, bled out with weapons in their hands. Three other heavily cybered bouncers grew stiff in great pools of blood and oil, and behind what was left of the bars, the beautiful bartenders had been carved up by streams of bullets, limbs akimbo and firearms resting near the fingertips of wherever their gun arm had ended up.

In his career in law enforcement, Julius had never seen a crime scene half this grisly. The firepower that WalCo had deployed here made the team that hit the FBI offices look like a Boy Scout squad armed with BB guns. That attack had been surgical—an attempt to take out the scientists and recapture or unleash the ooze monster. It would have been successful too, without Dr. Linden's quick thinking. This attack, though, was about nothing more than eradication; WalCo had detected a gangster digging into their secrets and had swatted that fly (along with whatever other flies happened to be nearby).

In Luther's office, the carnage continued. One last of the Speak Easy's augmented bouncers lay dead at the door's entrance. Bullets had reduced Fisk's beautiful desk to splinters, and behind it, where Julius expected to find the head gangster, he found instead only the Kalashnikov in a small pile of spent shell casings. Just past this, an open hatch in the floor, a steel portal downwards. A steel ladder embedded in the wall down. Julius didn't see anyone down there—had Luther escaped? Had the WalCo team let him go or chased after him?

They had left the rest of the room in shambles. Paintings on the walls had been torn off. Only charred carpet, plastic shrapnel, and bits of circuit boards remained where once a powerful computer had rested. WalCo covered its tracks with micro-explosives—no tech was recovering data here. But maybe Fisk was alive—maybe Julius could track him down before the WalCo black ops crew.

For the first time since arriving down here, Julius looked at Sierra. The paleness of her face and that sort of over-loaded vacant stare mirrored, he imagined, his own. It was time to return to the FBI offices and plan their next step—where would Fisk go? Could they track the remainder of the black ops team, or was it time to strike back? They knew where the WalCo facility was after all.

Two of the Vice agents were dispatched into the escape tunnel, and the rest of the Vice team would search the place for evidence. When the dust had settled, Julius noticed a missed call on his PCom.

When he flicked it to the holo, he found himself looking at the long blonde curls of Helen Spencer, his old partner's wife of five years. They'd only met a couple times, but he liked her. She'd made an honest man of Marcus. Now, her eyes glistened and her lower lip quivered. For a moment, Julius thought the playback had gotten stuck on the first couple seconds, but he confirmed that this was just part of the message. The playback timer read 18 seconds into the recording before Helen spoke.

"Julius, it's Helen Spencer, Marc's wife. I'm calling to let you know that Marc is dead. Gunned down in the street. They didn't even have the decency to rob him. Anyway, I know you two were close once, thought you might want to know we have services set up for Saturday next week. Would love for you to come."

He could see it in her eyes: Every word came as a battle. She shuddered as she spoke, but she got through the whole thing, severing the connection abruptly after inviting him. Julius stumbled over to an intact table in the middle of the Speak Easy and sat heavily on the raised stool. He stared at the floor, dark and slick with blood, but eventually the weight of his stare pulled through the floor, and he found himself staring deep into some void at the center of the Earth. Marcus, dead. Because of him, no doubt. Sierra stood nearby, politely giving him time to come to terms. Even if she hadn't felt it personally, she would be familiar with the notion that losing a partner—even a former partner—brought a unique sort of pain. One Julius had hoped never to experience again.

And yet, here it was. Only he didn't have time for it. He didn't have time to revisit the old haunts, go on a bender, pour one out for his old friend at the south pedestrian entrance to Arc 1 where they'd collared their first kidnapper trying to flee into the white all those years ago. He would make time soon—if he survived—but right now taking down WalCo was it. Was everything.

And Galloway and WalCo seemed to be panicking. An attack on the FBI offices, a scorched-earth attack on a lower slums club leaving over a dozen dead, and now they'd gunned down a security officer from a rival corporation all the way across the continent in Chicago. This frantic and widespread black ops action didn't match what Julius would expect from a simple cover-up. Sure, the ooze monster had killed three people. Sure, it was fucked up, and it would be a blow to profits and reputation if Julius and his team busted them for it. But this went way beyond cover-up. There were a dozen witnesses that had seen the ooze monster feeding on Petyr up in the viewing bay, so what were they even covering up?

No, this felt more like an existential threat. Something larger was at work behind the scenes, tied to the ooze monster. And Julius was going to nail Galloway to the wall for it.

They headed back to the Law Enforcement building, where Julius gathered Sierra and Linden in his office. He was just sitting down at his desk when his PCom rang again. The third of three very unexpected calls that day. With a glance at his two co-conspirators, Julius answered the call; "Director, this is not an exceptionally good time. What can I do for you?"

CHAPTER 19

❝ This is it, cards on the table."

The Director looked haggard, to say the least. Given the time difference between Alaska and Washington, he'd almost certainly been asleep when WalCo had hit the Arc 1 FBI office a few hours ago.

"I have an insider," the Director continued. "I don't know much about him, but he's been feeding me information. We're going to bring some law and order back to the corporations. Or at least to WalCo."

Julius looked at his feet. The ragged line of his pants barely extended past his knees. Dried blood spotted his skin and the black cloth, and the fresher blood of dead WalCo soldiers and Speak Easy goons caked the bottom half of his loafers. Sierra's cocktail dress, likewise, was spattered with blood from the shootout and oil from an ooze monster food fight. Linden looked his usual frumpy self, but two or three shades paler from his brush with murder and from the sights he'd seen at the Speak Easy. Quite a bunch they were.

"Director Taft, why didn't you say so sooner? You've been leading us around from the shadows instead of just telling us straight what's going on."

"At first, I didn't believe what I was hearing. Imagine, a remote-controlled ooze monster that eats people. I needed you to figure it out independently, before I could begin to trust my source. After that, well, I needed to lay low. My new assistant is a bought-and-paid-for WalCo spy, and I couldn't let him know I knew. I've found an excuse to send him away for a few hours, but this will be my last communication with you three until after your mission."

"Why don't you just throw him in prison?" Sierra asked.

"Because that would give the game away. Everything I've done is to preserve the element of surprise for you, now, in this moment."

"Sir, what do you mean?" Julius asked. "They had me bugged, they know everything I knew until a few hours ago."

"Which is why I held certain things back from you. They don't know that we know where their facility is located."

"Right here in Alaska!" Linden interrupted proudly.

The Director gave him a small smile and continued. "Yes, well done. I didn't know you'd figured it out already. In addition, they don't know that my inside source has a comprehensive blueprint of the facility, and that there's a way in that bypasses most of their security. They don't yet know that you're coming for them."

Julius and Sierra exchanged looks as the Director spoke. He could see it written in her eyes as much as he knew she saw it in his. Things were moving fast, and the ride was going to get turbulent before the day was done.

"If they knew these things, there would be a response team in the facility, and you'd never get close to your target. To preserve that element of surprise, we need to send you in now, and we need to send you in without mobilizing any other units. Otherwise, you don't stand a chance. The first line of defense for a facility like this is secrecy. They aren't equipped to stop you because they don't know you're coming."

"Who is our target, sir?" Julius asked.

The Director reached off screen, and the holodisplay flipped from the live feed of the man at his desk to a portrait of an older woman with long gray hair, in a lab coat. "This is nano-weapons specialist Dr. Olga Donskoy. WalCo imported her illegally from a

Soviet weapons research facility two years ago, and they've been putting her to work ever since. I don't have time to go into details, but her work has led to dozens of deaths in secret weapons tests around the world. We haven't been able to make anything stick, until now. Now we have evidence and testimony from my inside source. We know where she is, and we know you have a brief window to get in and extract her. I think we can get her to roll over on her masters, and if she names names higher up in WalCo, I think we can really do some good, get justice for –"

The Director paused, and the picture flipped back to his desk. He watched another screen just off-center from the squad before him. His brow furrowed and color drained from his face. Julius waited quietly for the briefing to continue.

"Dammit," the Director said. "We're out of time. They must have somehow intercepted our signal. My air traffic surveillance program has a dropship leaving a rapid response facility at the WalCo campus in Seattle, making directly for the Alaska facility. Two hours, and Dr. Donskoy will be dead or unreachable. I've requisitioned a shuttle and a pilot I trust. You've got to move fast. Bring the good doctor in, and I'll take it from there."

Julius's PCom buzzed, and then Sierra's and Linden's.

"Each of you has the file on Dr. Donskoy and the blueprint of the facility. The pilot knows where to go—she'll be dropping you outside a decommissioned maintenance tunnel. My insider has activated it again and dredged up the old access codes. From there, you'll move into the facility proper. You'll patch into the internal network, find Dr. Donskoy, and extract her before the response team arrives."

"Sir," Sierra said, "if they know we're coming now, won't she be protected? Maybe we should take a full team."

The Director shook his head. "This facility is dark—no communications, even with other WalCo facilities. They don't want people from outside knowing about it, and they don't want information from within making its way outside. Plus, we can't spare the manpower—we need a team to find Fisk, and we need another team to fortify the law enforcement building—if you're successful, there *will* be more attacks."

"If the facility is dark, how did your insider still manage to get word out to you?" Linden asked.

"For ten minutes every 24 hours, the Overseer of the facility can send out packets of information, to communicate with HQ. My insider managed to find a way in, to send his own transmissions during that window."

Now was Linden's opportunity to look uncomfortable. He shifted in his chair. "That's *very* high-level work, Director," Linden said. "I don't think I know a man alive capable of working at that level in that short a window."

The Director leaned forward. "Focus, people. One hour and fifty-five minutes left until that response team arrives at the WalCo facility. Our one and only window is closing: It's time for you three to get moving. Good luck and God speed."

With that, the call was over, the Director gone. The three of them were left sitting quietly in Julius's office, staring at each other. After a pause, they rose in near unison. Each of the men moved to his desk to grab some things while Sierra popped the clip out of her borrowed sidearm to check the ammo count.

"Can we bring the ooze monster, use it against the WalCo security team if we're found out?" Sierra asked.

Julius, rifling through his desk for additional ammo, stopped and looked up, awaiting Linden's response. That would be a hell of an asset.

Linden did not stop going through his own drawers. "No, I think that's out of the question. Even in the brief moment during which I took it over, the monster's progenitors nearly regained control of their creation. If we take it home, I'm sure they'll have plenty of safeguards. I believe that strategy would backfire."

"Maybe you need to stay behind, then, guide us from the base. I'm not sure risking you in the field is a good idea," Julius said.

Linden held up a small device of some sort, looked it over, and, satisfied, pocketed it. "You need me," he said, "to hack into their facility's security. You need me to understand what is or is not important evidence against this Dr. Donskoy. And I think you may find that I will be useful in a fight. I've got a few tricks of my own, in case we are attacked."

"He's right," Sierra said.

"Fine, but only because I'm very much enjoying this new and improved version of you, doctor," Julius said, sifting again through his desk, at last finding what he was looking for—a spare magazine for the sidearm Sierra had borrowed from him, and an ankle holster. He tossed her these, and then when Linden was done collecting gadgets, the three of them made for the elevator.

When they passed May Ellis' desk, she rose. "Where are you three off to now? Is everything okay? Is this all related to the attacks earlier?" She rapid-fired her questions too fast for anyone to answer them, and anyway they didn't have time.

Sierra elbowed Julius in the ribs, and her message was clear. He took a step closer to her. "May," he said.

"Yes?" she stopped mid-sentence.

"I can't go into all of this now. But when I get back, I'll tell you all about it. Over dinner?" He stumbled over the question at the end of it, now that he was this close to her and looking into her wide blue eyes, but he got it out.

When she smiled, he realized, it really lit the room. Bit of a cliché, sure, but if a thing was true, it was true. And this thing was true.

She quickly reined her smile in and scowled at him. "I *did* tell you to take it easy tonight, didn't I?"

"You did –" Julius started.

"But you're not going to, are you?" May Ellis interrupted.

Julius paused, considered his options here, and then shook his head.

She stared him down, and the time stretched out and he wished it would stretch forever, this eye contact, her attention warming him like a gentle sunbeam breaking through the storm above the Arc. But it did end after all.

"Well don't die out there, whatever you're going off to do," she said at last. "It wouldn't be right to pique my curiosity and offer me dinner only to die, you know."

"I'll try," he flashed his best cavalier smile, hoping that the seed of doubt—sprouted and growing as it was—didn't show through.

That was it then, time to get going. But this was good, this was a plan for success and a reason not to die, but to come back here to Arc 1 and keep living after all, his misgivings about the power of WalCo and their horrid Immortal enforcer aside. This was light at the end of the tunnel that was almost a suicide mission, normal life on the other side, waiting quietly for him with lovely red hair.

From there they were in the elevator and on their way. Ten minutes to the shuttleport if they hurried, ten more minutes waiting for clearance, and then they'd have about 90 minutes to find and break into a secret Arctic research facility. To get in and find the top-secret weapons researcher for the most powerful corporation on the North American west coast, extract her, and get away before more hired goons came gunning for them.

No problem, Julius thought. Right?

CHAPTER 20

"Buckle up."

Fortunately, Julius was already fully strapped into the shuttle's copilot seat, because the moment she said it, the Director's new pilot hit the thrusters. *Hard.* The shuttle careened from the launch pad directly through the narrow opening in the shuttleport bay, clearing Arc 1's dome in seconds.

Julius's heart leaped into his throat and then dropped into his stomach as the shuttle hit the Great White Spot at maximum acceleration. The blizzard raged, buffeting the shuttle with hurricane-force gusts of wind; thick clouds of snow lashed the cockpit window, limiting visibility to a few feet. The pilot seemed to be navigating purely based on radar.

Grunts from the passenger compartment were almost, but not quite, drowned out by the dueling roars of wind and engines. Julius hoped Linden had managed to get his air sickness bag deployed in time.

After a moment, the shuttle's speed stabilized, and the ride smoothed out a bit. There was still very little visibility, and the ship still rocked back and forth in the fury of the blowing wind, but Julius's heart returned to its normal position in his chest. He let out a great big breath he didn't realize he'd been holding.

The pilot turned to him and, smiling, let out a whoop. He looked back at her, trying his best to muster a smile of his own while pushing down the nausea. Sheng Xiaoli had clearly served in the Chinese military—the scars that criss-crossed her face told that story. Which conflict had been her last? She'd obviously deserted at some point but didn't seem to carry that heaviness of spirit that deserters normally did. He imagined the layers of her life for a moment—this person from the other side of the world, what sort of life had she lived?

All he knew was that the Director vouched for her, and she was clearly comfortable in the cockpit; that was more than enough.

"So, what's the mission?" Xiaoli asked.

Julius said nothing at first. What had the Director told her?

"I know, I know," she said. "Secret mission. Reuben was very cryptic."

Reuben? She knew the director by first name?

"I just need to know what to expect out here," she said.

"Fair enough," Julius said. "I assume the Director gave you a destination and told you to hurry. We're racing another shuttle to that location. We'll possibly be in a firefight with WalCo private security while inside, and we'll be coming out hot with a prisoner to extract. I don't know if the destination facility has any anti-aircraft capabilities, but I assume not, or the Director would hopefully have informed us."

"Sure, if he knew about them, he would've. Would've told me, too."

Julius sat back and digested that. How good was the Director's insider? WalCo had nearly unlimited resources, and obviously a deep concern for the secrecy of this facility. Could they have anti-aircraft guns? Air combat drones? It was too late to worry about those things, now. All he could do was hope for the best, and trust in this mysterious pilot that Director Taft had connected them with, and the mysterious insider at the facility that had made all of this possible. It was an awful lot of mystery, but what choice did any of them have?

They rode in silence for some minutes, the cold wind singing to him through the seams in the ship's plating.

Something hit the shuttle roof with a "clunk," impossibly loud. And then another something, white and the size of a bowling ball, smashed into the plexi-plastic of the cockpit window, cracking it so far and so wide across the co-pilot's side that Julius thought it might cave in altogether, pinning him to his seat and ending his life.

"Hail," Xiaoli said. "*Wo cao.*" She jerked the ship to the left, broke hard, and then threw the shuttle into a steep dive.

Julius white-knuckled the armrests and forced a ragged breath through his clenched jaw.

A few more impacted the roof, a slow staccato at first, and then the frozen ice came cascading from the sky. Two more cracks quickly sprouted on the cockpit, and the noise from the roof was so deafening that Julius thought the whole ship might be torn apart.

Until the shuttle pulled up sharply, just beside a tower of a snow dune—more of a pillar of ice really—and the hail went silent. The engine hummed quietly, and they hovered in place.

"What'd you do?" Julius asked.

"The hail is blowing west to east, so I put us in hover-mode on the east side of a great big snow dune. The hail will pass shortly, it always does out here."

"How did you even know this dune was here?" Julius asked.

She gestured casually at the sensor panel. "Always pay attention to the terrain below when flying in a storm."

"And you processed all that in less than five seconds?" Julius said.

Xiaoli shrugged. "Normally I'd be flying above the storm, but the Director wants us flying low and fast. Stealth mission. Gotta be ready for anything, flying inside the Great White Spot."

This was bad. Good that she'd saved them, clearly, she was a competent pilot. But the response team was gaining on them. Every minute they hovered in place was one less minute that they'd have to navigate the facility and nab Dr. Donskoy.

"How long until we're back underway? We're on a very unfriendly timeline here."

Xiaoli scowled at him. "I'm not a weather girl, I'm a shuttle pilot. Do you want me to just fly through the hail and hope for the best?"

"No, we're no good to anyone if we die halfway to the facility."

"What's going on?" Sierra said, poking her head into the cockpit. "Why are we stopped? And holy shit, what happened to the windshield?"

"'Hail,' is the answer to all of your questions," Xiaoli said, shaking her head and checking some of her displays.

"*Hail?*" Sierra asked.

"Bowling ball sized hail," Julius said, shifting in his seat to look more squarely at Sierra, holding his hands apart to show her.

"I've heard it on the roof of the Arc before, but –" she started.

"Time to be seated, storm's almost over," Xiaoli said.

Sierra nodded and stepped back into the passenger area. Julius could hear her talking in low tones, presumably explaining things to Dr. Linden.

In the unexpected silence Julius felt a void open in his mind. Between the drinking and the date and the attacks on the FBI office and the Speak Easy and the sudden call from the Director, his brain had been under constant bombardment for days. Now all of that drained into the sudden lull, the eye of the storm that his life had become.

In that void appeared a vision of his parents. His mother, an Egyptian banker, beautiful with her long, braided hair. And his father, an ex-football star turned cop, forced into early retirement when Baltimore's city government folded and turned over law enforcement duties to the various corporate jurisdictions. He had never forgiven them for abandoning him, but he saw it clearly in their eyes now: a primal kind of fear. They weren't leaving him behind for that colony ship bound for Titan, they were just escaping at all costs. Even him.

And then though he never thought of forgiveness, he did imagine himself in another spacecraft on approach to Titan. From this distance, the moon appeared a smooth amber orb, a greenish atmospheric haze just coming into view on the fringe. Behind it, colossal Saturn loomed, the alien arc of its cold rings sandy, rose, white, shimmering in the distance.

He couldn't see it yet, but he knew that soon the shuttle would touch down on a landing pad outside a small arcology, home to about five hundred colonists. His parents waited there; arms outstretched in hopeful reunion. A peaceful life of repairing air scrubbers and water filters awaited him there. He relaxed into the chair and let out a small sigh of relief.

Without warning Xiaoli hammered down on the accelerator, the shuttle lurching forward, the wind rocking them and Julius's whole body coiling and his fingers digging into the arm rest and the blizzard howling and howling through the seams in the shuttle. Had Sierra had time enough to be seated? There were no sounds of distress from back there, she must have.

The hail had passed and there were no further obstructions. They soared over an Alaskan tundra obscured by the thrashing winds of the Great White Spot, and Julius watched the flickering passage of their tiny blip on a tiny radar map approaching a blank space with a green circle around it that represented the hidden facility. They arrived sooner than he expected.

Julius squinted into the white, could not see anything below them, no facility, no ground. He looked to Xiaoli for confirmation. She did not look happy. And then red warning bulbs lit up all around the cockpit, and the ship's computer spoke for the first time.

Xiaoli closed her eyes. "*Cao ni ma*, Reuben," she said, looking up at Julius after a long pause. "There are four missile batteries locked on to our ship's heat signature. We're dead."

CHAPTER 21

"Unidentified craft, you are trespassing in private airspace. Divert immediately," the smooth AI voice demanded.

Xiaoli looked at Julius. "I'm good. I'm damn good. But those are Faerie Fire missile batteries—heat-tracking, multi-directional, proximity detonated plasma warheads. Maybe if we were in a fighter craft of some kind, we could at least outrun them."

"We've come this far," Julius started.

"But we can't go any further. I'm going to turn us around," Xiaoli said. "If we're lucky they're really giving us the choice."

"Unidentified craft, you have five seconds to divert, or ellllllse...." The voice seemed to deactivate halfway through, trailing into fragmented static. At the same time, the red warning lights ceased.

"Ms. Sheng?" Julius said.

"Lock is broken. It seems the missiles have deactivated."

"What changed?" Julius asked, the question hanging in the suddenly too-quiet air.

The comms crackled to life again, this time the voice robotic, weirdly stilted, with the emphasis on the wrong words. Like one of the primitive talk-to-text programs from the past century that kids liked to trot out from time to time for the giggles.

"Special Agent Julius Weaver, Shangwei Sheng Xiaoli," the voice started.

"*Former*," Xiaoli interrupted. "Dishonorable discharge," she said with a measure of pride.

It continued on, as though she had not spoken. "I have deactivated the base defense systems, external and internal. Human security is very limited, so you should have relatively little difficulty apprehending Dr. Donskoy."

"Who are you?" Julius asked, leaning forward.

"I am Director Reuben Taft's inside source."

"Yes, I figured as much. But *who are you?*"

After a long pause, the answer came back. "You should hurry, time is limited."

"Everyone's got to be a mystery," Xiaoli said. "*Ben dan,*" she muttered under her breath. The ship shuddered as she took it out of neutral and brought them quickly to ground level. They landed gently, the ship shifting slightly on the hard-packed ice beneath.

Finally, Julius could see their destination. Maybe fifty feet in front of him, a chrome-colored bubble nestled like a blister amidst thick white snowdrifts. A surprisingly large facility—kept secret by little more than its location and the frequency with which the storm presumably obscured visual discovery by wide lens spy satellites. Closest to them stood a small door, a keypad beside it. They were here.

"Keep the engine running, Ms. Sheng," Julius said, unbuckling himself.

"Good luck," she said. "I have a feeling you'll need it."

In the passenger compartment, Sierra and Linden were already zipping up in the arctic suits the Director had provided for them. Julius had one too, form-fitting and warm. He dressed as quickly as he could, moving his gun belt to the outside of the gear.

It took less than two minutes, but those two minutes were precious. Should they have dressed before landing? It was too late now, time to move. He pulled the thermal hood up and over his head and ears.

Weapon drawn, Julius hit the button for the shuttle's passenger exit and the doors opened, the ramp extending to the tundra below. They stepped into the storm. The wind whipped at him, cutting through even the heavy-duty thermal lining of his new gear. The snow blew into his eyes, and he shielded them against the fury of the blizzard with his free hand. Out here the howling wind transformed into the guttural roar of a monstrous beast. It burrowed into him, and it latched on, and it ripped at his guts. This was not a place for human beings. Fortunately, they were close to the door, to shelter. He trudged forward, the snowpack like concrete beneath the thick synth-leather of his thermal boots. Linden and Sierra followed.

In the raging storm, they chose each step with deliberate care. For a moment Julius walked in a dust storm on Titan, kitted in a fully sealed exo-suit. A gust blew so hard that it almost lifted Julius into the air. When he turned back to the others, he saw that it had actually blown Linden over. Sierra helped him up. One foot at a time, they pressed forward.

After what seemed like ages, they reached the door. Julius pulled up the codes on his wrist display, accessing the PCom files the Director had sent them earlier, and punched them into the keypad. The door scraped open, the shriek of metal on metal rising even above the howling winds. This door had not been used in quite some time. How long had the facility been here, hidden in the white? He stepped in.

Julius moved further in to make room for the others, and the door slid shut behind them, leaving them in darkness. At first, he thought his eyes just needed time to adjust from the brilliance of the all-white world behind them, but when Linden activated the flashlight function on his PCom, he realized that there were simply no lights on in this space. Of course, it was a disused maintenance tunnel. Why would they waste energy to illuminate it? Sierra flipped her light on, and Julius followed suit.

They stood in a smallish hallway, piping and wiring exposed to the open air. Nothing decorative, no signs or displays to guide a prospective traveler through this space. But there was only one way forward, and so they moved further into the facility. They passed through about a hundred feet of tunnel, before coming to a fork. Left, right, and a door in the center. A computer screen mounted in the wall just to the side flickered to life when they approached. Motion sensors? Or was the insider somehow watching them? Julius looked around, but it was too dark to see if there were any cameras installed.

"Allow me," Linden said, stepping forward.

Julius moved aside, and turned to Sierra while the scientist went to town on the facility's systems. "I have a weird feeling about all of this. It feels like a trap."

"I'm not happy with the mysterious insider angle," she said, "but if WalCo were trying to kill us, they would've blown us out of the air with those missiles."

He shrugged. "You're right, but it just feels wrong. Something's off."

"Okay," Linden said.

"That was fast," Sierra said, leaning in.

"This newer and more confident Dr. Linden is getting things done," Julius said, slapping the smaller man on the back in a gesture that almost knocked him over.

"I've done a lot this week that I never would have dreamed I was capable of," he started.

"Guys," Sierra said. "This is great and all, but we're on the clock here."

Julius agreed and turned to the newly hacked terminal. On the screen were digital blueprints of the facility. Every room had a label super-imposed, describing the room's functionality. The display had been centered on a blinking red dot, static in a location called "nano-research center 2."

"It seems that WalCo have chipped their scientists," Linden said. "We'll have to find a way to scramble the chip once we get Dr.

Donskoy, unless we want WalCo chasing us back to the Director. But for now, it should make it exceedingly easy to find her. Looks like she's working right now."

Julius reached over and swiped the map display onto his own PCom, pulling it up on his wrist display.

Linden reached over and pointed. "We are here."

Not too far to go, then. Straight through the door and down a couple of hallways, and they'd have Donskoy. Hopefully they didn't run into a lot of other base personnel.

"Can you get this door open for us, Doctor?" Sierra asked.

"Absolutely..." Linden started, trailing off quickly as the screen display flashed through a few different menus, and the door slid open.

"That wasn't you." Julius wasn't asking. They were definitely being watched by the Director's insider. He only hoped the person behind the screen was really on their side.

On the other side of the doors, things looked very different. The smooth metal corridors had been properly finished: no exposed wires, gentle LED lighting installed in the walls on either side, with thin bands of colored lights that presumably led to different portions of the facility for those who did not have a map on hand or became easily lost. Pretty standard stuff. No people in sight.

"Shall we?" Sierra said, stepping through with gun drawn. Julius and Linden came close behind.

They followed the map without issue. Past the dining hall and living quarters they went, around a corner past the infirmary and a number of small research labs devoted to what the map would describe as anything from "bio-mechanics" to "cybernetic enhancements." They were evidently in the human enhancement wing of the facility. A booming commercial field for any corporation—not as much research needed, but there would always be tweaks and advances, new features and so forth—so where were the people?

Past these, they moved into the heavy hitting research areas, the big scientific frontiers. Nano-machines, microbial research. Things that were too tiny to see were the hardest to defend against, and consequently the biggest ticket items in corporate warfare and espionage.

Sure enough, as soon as they cleared the double doors connecting the two wings, they saw a human member of security, armed and armored. Only he didn't approach them or radio in for backup. Of course, he couldn't do those things—he was dead. Face down in a pool of his own blood, skin pale, he seemed to have just toppled over and bled out through his eyes, mouth, and ears.

They stepped quietly around the body, moving towards their objective. Was everyone dead, was that why they hadn't met any resistance? Was this the Director's insider? Donskoy hadn't moved, was she dead too? She was no good to them dead. Julius pushed aside these questions. Nothing to do now but move further in, hope for the best. Stay on guard.

His finger tensed on his trigger finger as they rounded the next corner. Closer and closer to Donskoy. Two more bodies here—an older man in a lab coat and another security guard—slumped on the ground, skin pallid, eyes bloodshot, contents of their veins and arteries emptied onto the stainless-steel floors. Something was very wrong. But they were close to Donskoy. They had to extract her, and then they could sort out what had gone wrong later.

"Dr. Linden," Sierra said, "any ideas what's going on here?"

"Some kind of pathogen would be my first guess, but these people obviously died almost immediately. Nothing known to us has such rapid onset of death. Maybe a chemical weapon, but such a thing would have already killed us, as well."

"Comforting," Julius said. "But barring an imminent threat to us or the mission, let's keep the speculation down until we have what—who—we came for. Donskoy's just down the hall here."

The map led them on a winding path to a locked door. Just on the other side was their target. The head scientist in charge of creating that horrific ooze monster, the one responsible for the deaths of three citizens of Arc 1, the person who set in motion the chain of events that led to the deaths of three civilians and five members of the FBINA, gunned down in their own office. He breathed slow and steady, reaching for the door controls.

The door wasn't just locked, it had been jammed shut. Linden stepped up and tapped at a few buttons.

"Donskoy's hacked the door's controls. She's also isolated the room's life support functions, for some reason. Maybe this is a pathogen after all?"

"Yet as you said, we're fine," Julius said. "Should we have some kind of biohazard gear on?"

Linden rubbed his neck nervously. "Anything that's loose in here, we're already exposed. And judging from the condition of the dead we've found, if it *is* a pathogen, it would have killed us almost instantly."

"Ultimately, it's too late to gear up for a biohazard, and anyway, we didn't bring anything like that. All we can do is hope we aren't affected," Sierra said.

"Agreed. Linden, can you force your way through?" Julius asked.

"It looks like our insider has tried a number of tricks already but let me take a look." Linden tapped away for a few minutes, to no avail. The door remained shut and the minutes ticked off the clock.

"Wait, if the insider was here trying to get this door open, where did they go?" Sierra asked.

Julius looked around. The hallway had a few other doors, and dead-ended in an emergency exit. The exit hadn't been tampered with, so he went door to door while Linden worked on getting in to Donskoy. Mostly they were empty labs. A couple more dead scientists had slumped over while looking in microscopes or collapsed to the floor besides now-shattered beakers or test-tubes. No living person, or any sign that one had passed this way.

"I don't know," Julius said. "But we're running out of time, so that's just going to have to be one more mystery for another day."

"Nothing standard worked for our insider, I can see signs that he tried a variety of digital hacks to crack this door open—Donskoy was too smart for him. But he never tried a hard approach. I don't think he ever came here physically. It was all remote. Anyway, I've got a few custom options." As he spoke, Linden pulled out one of his gadgets, a little metal disc laced with orange wires. He cracked open the computer's internals, pulling out some wiring, and spliced in his device. "This will communicate with the door's base programming, rewriting it with code from a standard space station template. Tells the door that there's an oxygen deficiency in the sealed room, emergency fail-safes will kick in that should override any other locking or blocking program, and open sesame."

"That's a very wonderful and very specific toy you've brought with you," Sierra said.

"Oh, it's not that specific," Linden said, tapping commands into the display, which had changed schemes after he finished splicing his device in. "Most of these kinds of secure doors share some basic hardware and code. 80% of them are manufactured by WalCo subsidiaries. It's practically a universal skeleton key. Never know when you'll need to get in somewhere. And that... should be that."

At the second "that" the door slid open, and there was Dr. Donskoy, standing at a microscope. She looked up, startled by the noise of the door, and the look of horror that transfixed her face froze Julius in place.

"What have you done to me?" she asked, taking one step forward, before stumbling to her knees. When she rose again, her eyes were already bloodshot. "I could have stopped it, but now that you're here to carry it, there's no stopping it, is there?" She coughed up blood into her hand and wiped it dismissively on her apron. "You idiots have no idea –" she started, but before she could finish, she convulsed, and her body shuddered once. It almost looked as though she was stretching after a long sleep. And then before Julius or the others could react, she collapsed to the floor. Blood seeped from every orifice. Sierra checked her pulse, but Julius knew she was dead.

"Don't touch her," Linden cried, but Sierra already had her finger to the woman's neck. After a moment, she shook her head. Fear and disgust warred with each other on her face, and Julius imagined the same for his own. He was paralyzed. What had happened? What had killed Donskoy but spared his team? What did they do now?

Flashing orange warning lights jarred Julius back into the here and now. The facility had been stone silent while everyone within died of... something. But now came warning lights? A voice—the same stilted old voice-to-text—announced the reason.

Warning, facility enacting Scorched Earth protocol. Estimated time until detonation of facility 10 minutes. Please evacuate.

CHAPTER 22

Julius tried Xiaoli on the short-wave radio band connecting their PComs for the mission. Nothing. He tried calling the Director. Nothing, jammed. No signals going out, but it all pointed to one thing. The response team was here, blocking distress calls from getting out, and blowing the building. Did they know what was going on inside? Something killing everyone? They surely didn't plan to let Julius's team escape alive. He hoped they hadn't gotten to Xiaoli yet.

"Do you think you can communicate with the insider?" Julius asked, looking to Linden.

"Short of shouting into the air and hoping he hears us, no."

Nine minutes until facility destruction.

"I believe it's time to leave, Special Agent Weaver," Sierra said, voice strained.

"Yes," Julius said, looking around the room for something—anything—they could use. He didn't want to leave empty-handed.

"Julius!" Sierra shouted.

He looked up at her. "We have a couple minutes. Run through it with me." He spoke fast but tried to keep his voice level. Remain calm, work the case. "The Director's insider leads us here to apprehend a nano-weapons specialist, takes down the defenses to let us in."

"Oh, we're going to die," Linden interrupted.

"Please focus, doctor," Julius said. "There's still time, and I need you."

Linden nodded, wiping sweat from his forehead.

"Once we are inside, base personnel start dropping dead. We break through, get to Donskoy, the one the insider originally clued us into, and she drops dead in seconds. What causes this? Doctor, you said it looked like a pathogen, but worked too fast. And it hasn't affected us. What does that sound like to you?"

"Nano-machines," he said, seemingly surprised.

"It's all about nano-machines," Sierra jumped in. "The ooze monster with a nano-machine brain, the surveillance bugs on your eyes, and now this thing, killing everyone on the base."

"But why?" Julius asked. "What's the motivation for bringing us here to watch every potential suspect die a horrible death, and then sparing our lives?"

"A terror attack that needed witnesses?" Sierra asked.

Eight minutes until facility destruction.

"Can we discuss this later, *please*?" Linden said.

Julius looked around the room. What had Donskoy been working on? He looked in the microscope that she was using. Something that could've been a cell, or a nano-machine, or a speck of dust, he didn't know. He stood back. He was going about this wrong, he didn't have the necessary tools to do this alone. They were scared, but they would help him.

"Okay, we don't have a lot of time here. Linden, download and grab any data that you can on what Donskoy was working on. Sierra, do you think you can patch into the system and check for anyone still living? If this insider is really responsible, odds are good he's trying to escape. I want to find him."

"If everyone is chipped, as the Dr. Linden says, I'll find him," she said.

Seven minutes until facility destruction.

They went to work. Julius stood in the middle of the room and closed his eyes. Ooze monsters. Nano-machines. WalCo. A remote-controlled killing machine being used to commit murder, and then a mysterious researcher in a private weapons facility leading the FBI around by its nose. Coincidence? No such thing. So, what if it was the insider that hacked the ooze monster? Then this was all an elaborate plot to lead FBI agents to a facility full of nothing but dangerous secrets, and Julius had played right into the hands of a killer. But who wanted him here badly enough to commit murder, and *why*?

"Linden," Julius said. "What other projects was WalCo working on in this facility?"

Linden stood up from downloading files onto his PCom and pulled up some notes on the facility itself. Read from the list quickly, voice stuttering and eyes fluttering.

"Nanotechnology, weaponized microbial research, human enhancement, plasma and gauss weaponry advancements, bio-synthetic compound fabrication, AI weapons systems, quantum processor micronization, fusion system miniaturization –" he was prepared to go on, but the countdown interrupted.

Four minutes until base destruction.

"What happened to six and five minutes?" Julius asked.

"We had those while you were standing there zoning out," Sierra said.

Shit. They were running out of time. He had some ideas, but not enough evidence. If he could just—

"Okay," Sierra said. "Nobody left alive in here but us. No insider to bring in. I don't know what happened, but I know we're not dying here. Dr. Linden and I are leaving. Are you coming with us, Agent Weaver?"

"Yes," Julius said, without hesitation. It was time to go.

And so, they ran. Back down the corridors, over the blood-pool bodies in the hallways.

"We'll figure it out later," Linden huffed. "I downloaded a lot of files from the nano-tech database. I got every file cross-referencing the bio-synthetic compound fabrication department, which should definitely include the data on our ooze monster."

"We'll get them," Sierra agreed. "We just have to get out alive first."

Around the corner, and they were back into the dark of the maintenance tunnel. They flipped their lights on and careened through, finally reaching the door to the exterior.

Two minutes until base destruction.

The door slid open, the crushing white radiance of the sun and the snow blinding Julius as he stumbled out into the cold. The door closed behind the three of them.

Julius heard the man before he saw him, one of several hazy shapes slowly resolving in his vision. A familiar voice, deep and coarse, dripping with impatience and sharp with contempt for the world. A voice that, even shouting against the howling blizzard, seemed so quietly dangerous that Julius briefly considered fleeing back into the imminently exploding research facility.

"I'm very disappointed, Special Agent Weaver. I'm quite certain I made it clear that I didn't want to come back to Alaska."

His eyes adjusted sufficiently, Julius could now see Galloway standing between him and the shuttle. Beside the white-eyed Immortal stood six WalCo agents kitted out in black tactical gear and armed to the teeth. A seventh and an eighth were at the shuttle door with plasma torches, trying to cut their way in. Xiaoli hadn't left yet, but she'd surely make a run for it before they got the door open.

"And yet, here I am," Galloway continued. "And here you are. Escaping from an off-books WalCo private research facility that you should not even know about, mere moments after I received a distress call breaking an ironclad radio-silence protocol, that merely shows the base overseer dying, blood pouring from his eyes. It seems everyone is dead inside and here you are, trying to escape."

"If you try anything, the Director of—"

"Reuben Taft is dead. Suicide, apparently," Galloway interrupted. From his tone it was clear that this was no suicide. That bastard of an assistant, the spy, had probably arranged the whole thing.

"What do you want from us?" Sierra asked.

In response, he held his hand up, one finger. Wait.

The ground shook, and just behind them, the facility crumpled inward and then imploded completely. Julius could just barely see a dim flash of fire from beneath the ground, and then the nearby maintenance shaft and every other visible section of the base was sucked into a roiling inferno. The ground shuddered and Julius struggled to keep his feet as a mere handful of yards away, the sudden detonation seemed to pull the air into the firestorm.

It stopped as quickly as it began, leaving a deep chasm where moments ago there had been a building. Julius teetered on his feet, awed by the fact that he had not been sucked into the conflagration. He looked to Sierra and Linden to confirm that they were in fact both still standing as well. They were.

Some bomb. It wouldn't have given off any kind of light or sound that a spy satellite could track but had completely eradicated the facility. Only a handful of people would ever know what had gone on here.

He turned back to Galloway.

"That was every bit as spectacular as I hoped," Galloway said, smiling. "It's important to relish the beautiful little moments in life, don't you think?" He looked from the smoking crater back to Sierra. "Now, young lady, to answer your question. I want you to die. You are the last loose end to tie up."

"You can't just kill us," she said.

"Of course I can," he said. "Though it may be little comfort to you in your final moments, your death will avert a global disaster the likes of which we have never seen and from which we could not hope to recover."

He raised his sidearm, and the six agents on each side of him tensed, ready to fire. Galloway smiled and closed his eyes, clearly relishing this moment as well.

"It's the simple things," he said to nobody in particular.

"Get down, close your eyes, and wait for three," Linden said. It was almost a whisper, just loud enough for the three of them to hear over the roaring storm. He reached into his pack, and quicker than you'd have thought, he tossed a small metal device into the air, in the general direction of the response team.

Julius did not wait to see; he did as the scientist bid. He hit the snow, and he closed his eyes. There was a deafening bang and piercing flash of light behind his eyes. Like a neo-plasma-flashbang. His ears rang.

Odd that the doctor was packing standard military hardware. And what had he meant, wait for three? Julius kept his eyes closed.

Another bang, and another flash. And then a third, after another few seconds. Julius grinned. That's what Linden had meant. He opened his eyes and rose. The flashbang hadn't been a flashbang at all, not in the conventional sense. It hovered in the air a few more seconds, wisps of smoke rising from the tiny drone, before dropping to the snowpack, spent. The response team were scattered, rolling in the snow in clear agony.

The other two WalCo agents had abandoned their work on the shuttle and were approaching with weapons drawn when the ramp dropped to the snow and there were two muzzle-flashes from within. The two agents dropped dead, and there was Xiaoli behind them, sidearm in hand, gesturing frantically at the team.

Julius checked behind him. Nothing but a smoldering crater. His team would have to get past the WalCo agents before they recovered to escape. Linden and Sierra were already moving, and so he did too. They did their best to hustle, pushing against the weight of the wind with each step.

They clambered past the stunned agents. Already the men in masks were stirring. The triple flash of the device had been enough to overwhelm even the advanced optic mods of a man like Galloway, but it would not be long until they recovered. Already algorithms in tiny cyber-eyes were over-writing the static and returning all systems to normal. Julius considered drawing his weapon, but was he really going to execute seven stunned WalCo agents? He pointed his weapon at Galloway, but before he could pull the trigger, the Immortal seemed to shrug off his blindness, and pointed his own sidearm at Julius, firing off several frantic shots.

They went wide, but the whole black ops team was stirring. Julius ducked out of the way of Galloway's shots and continued towards the shuttle. They were too disoriented to hit him at anything but point-blank range, but that wouldn't last long.

The FBI team pressed on towards the shuttle. When they were maybe a dozen yards from away, Julius realized they weren't going to make it. They could only continue to trudge through thick snow drifts, but the agents were recovering, crawling to their knees and preparing to rise. The storm might slow people, but it wouldn't slow down bullets.

Julius stopped. "Go," he roared at Sierra and Linden. "Tell everyone you can what happened here, get the word out. Do what you can to get justice for everyone."

"Don't be so melodramatic," Linden shouted back. "We're not leaving without you."

"Of course we are," Sierra said, grabbing Linden and dragging him away. "Someone has to stand and fight so you can escape with the data. And we don't have time to argue about whether it's me or him."

"Thank you," Julius started to say, but she was already moving away, out of earshot in the howling storm.

When he turned, the WalCo agents were rising to their feet. The Immortal was already on his feet, shaking his head as though to clear it. A clean shot. Julius took it, squeezing the trigger three times. Right as he fired, a gust of wind hit him hard in the side. The second and third shots went wide, but the first hit the evil bastard in the shoulder, dropping him back to the snow. The response team fell prone, taking what little cover they could in the snow.

Julius went to one knee, firing over their heads quickly enough to keep them down, but slowly enough to conserve ammo. He just needed to buy his team a handful of seconds.

The operatives were rolling apart, spacing their positions so some of them could get their heads out of the snow and fire back without exposing themselves. He was about done. He checked his weapon's tiny ammo display on the bottom of the magazine. Three shots left. He took them, and then looked back. Sierra and Linden were boarding the shuttle. She stopped and looked back at him, and then the ramp slid closed, and the ship took off quickly.

When Julius turned again, all six of the WalCo agents had their weapons trained on him. He took a very deep breath and dropped his empty sidearm onto the Arctic snowpack. He was ready to die.

"Hold your fire," Galloway said, rising once again to his feet. His shoulder had already stopped bleeding, a nano-gel growing across the gunshot wound even as Julius watched. "I want to take him back alive."

"Torture?" Julius asked. His heart beat rapidly. They'd done it. His team had escaped. Donskoy was dead, but they had reams of data on illegal weapons research. They had the Director's files, and they had enough evidence of murder-by-ooze-monster to bring the case to trial. The FBI was toothless compared to a mega-corporation like WalCo, but murdering the Director of the entire FBI North America branch was too much, even for WalCo. There would be repercussions. The team had done it, whatever *it* was. They'd won. They had achieved... well, something at least. *Someone* would have to go to jail, and WalCo would lose millions.

And now Julius would answer to an evil maniac with nothing left to lose. He looked around for ways to end his own life. If only he'd saved a bullet for himself.

"Torture? No," Galloway said. "Worse. I'm going to lock you up with a 24-hour newsfeed. Everything that happens next, it will be your fault." When he spoke, his voice wavered. Was that fear? "I want you to watch. Watch as it all unravels."

The blue flames of Xiaoli's shuttle flickered in the hazy white fog of the raging blizzard for a moment, and then they were gone. Back to the world, back to safety. Back to Arc 1. What was in there with them that even a man like this feared? A pathogen, the thing responsible for killing all the base's inhabitants? No, they'd all be dead.

One of the operatives grabbed Julius' gun off the ground, and another cuffed his hands behind his back. They hauled him to his feet and began to walk him back to their shuttle.

If not a pathogen, was it something else? Something unrelated hidden away in the laundry list of dangerous and illegal activity that WalCo had undertaken here? He felt it at his mind's edge, waiting for him to reach out and grasp it. His subconscious had already figured this out, so it fell only to his conscious mind to catch up. What was that laundry list? Nanotechnology, weaponized microbial research, human enhancement, plasma and gauss weaponry advancements, bio-synthetic compound fabrication, AI weapons systems... he paused.

AI weapons systems. A mysterious insider that controlled nano-machines, performed herculean feats of hacking that Linden thought impossible, and didn't seem ever to be physically present in the research facility before it imploded. Nano-machines that could land on your body without you knowing it, take a ride to wherever you were going. Especially if you were going to civilization, to a city with a million unrestricted access points to the web. A few nanoseconds to leap from Arc 1 to the net, and from there to any networked PCom, custom rig, cybernetic limb, coffee shop payment processor, janitor bot or any other of a billion digital devices around the globe.

"Galloway," Julius said, looking back. "Did your people create a rogue AI here at this base? Is that what brought us here? Is that what's on the shuttle with my people right now, hitching a ride on invisible nano-machines?"

Galloway said nothing, staring fiercely straight ahead, but Julius' gut told him he was right. Some rogue AI was hitching a ride back to civilization with his people right now, and that terrified Galloway. It terrified Julius too.

A storm was coming to Arc 1, to May Ellis and everyone else in the city and beyond. A cold wind that would sweep down from the north, and sorrow would follow with it. And Julius would only be able to sit and watch from a WalCo cell as the world unraveled.

Acknowledgements

This prequel to *Colossus* owes much to many, and I will endeavor to acknowledge and thank all of you! As I said in the acknowledgements for that book, if your name doesn't make it onto this list, please forgive me, and know you have my deepest gratitude for the thing or things you did that helped me become the Greg I am in this universe.

First, of course, my wife and parents, who have both supported me and kept me alive for many, many years now. You know what you mean to me, or ought to.

Special thanks, also, to my girls. Juno and Zelda: A net 37 pounds worth of vicious and loving attack dogs. Thanks for keeping the neighbors in line, and keeping the cheese supply in the house from getting out of hand. And of course for being excellent therapy dogs and professional menaces, despite a total lack of special training.

I am blessed to have amazing in-laws. John and Mary Jo; Lynn; Austin, Cassie, and little Wesley. I cherish our time together, and am unendingly grateful for your love and support. A family should be a protective cocoon or a shield against the world, but often proves to be just the opposite. I beat pretty long odds marrying into this one.

Brandon "Batman" Getz, champion editor and friend, thank you for your professional editing skills, without which this book would be a grave disappointment to all of my former teachers. It's pretty heroic that you're able to invest the time to edit my work while also raising two kids alongside their beautiful mother, working a day job, and doing your own writing.

Olivia Croom-Hammerman, AKA the Croom-Hammer, who never weighed in on her nickname last time. Olivia, you're an exceptional book designer. Thank you for finding time to work on my little novella despite growing an entire human person inside you this fall. The kid's going to be a rockstar.

A special thank you to Betty Elgyn, which is the online name/persona of the artist who created the hardcover art both for this book, and for *Colossus*. Betty, thanks for lending me your artistic talent. Thanks for being responsive and professional and amazing despite being at the epicenter of an unjust war. Слава Україні. бережи себе.

Last, but far from least, an emphatic thanks to Heather Bacani. Heather, the amount of support I received from you since the release of *Colossus* is out of this world. For a friend of my wife from years back to take the time to leave my book a review on THREE different platforms, share kind words with me personally, and THEN volunteer to be a beta reader for *Cold Wind Blowing...* I was and still am blown away.

About the Author

Greg Leunig lives in Kansas City Missouri with his wife and two dogs, in a household powered almost entirely by cheese and naps. His day job involves saving the world AKA chipping away at the megalithic US coal and oil industry AKA he is in solar. He has a Master of Fine Arts Degree in Creative Writing, despite which he prefers to write about magic and robots and monsters and explosions.

Greg's fiction and poetry have variously appeared in Daily Science Fiction, Apex Magazine, Strange Horizons, and others. His first novel, *Multipocalypse*, appeared in serial form on the now-defunct Jukepop Serials, and his second, *Colossus*, was released by Spaceboy Books in 2022. Learn more about Greg's work at https://pleasefeedthesquirrels.com/.

Nate Ragolia is a lifelong lover of science fiction and its power to imagine worlds more hopeful and inclusive than the real one. His first book, *There You Feel Free*, was published by 1888's Black Hill Press in 2015. Spaceboy Books reissued it in 2021. He's also the author of *The Retroactivist* (2017). His most recent book, *One Person Can't Make a Difference* (2022), was featured on Tor.com's Can't Miss Indie Press Speculative Fiction list, and was translated into Italian for Ringworld Sci-Fi in 2023. He founded and edited *BONED*, a literary magazine, and also created two webcomics. Nate is also a husband and a dog dad.

Shaunn Grulkowski has been compared to Warren Ellis and Phillip K. Dick and was once described as what a baby conceived by Kurt Vonnegut and Margaret Atwood would turn out to be. He's at least the fifth best Slavic-Latino-American sci-fi writer in the Baltimore metro area. He's the author *Retcontinuum*, and the editor of *A Stalled Ox* and *The Goldfish* for 1888/Black Hill Press.